CLEVE F. ADAMS

has also written

SABOTAGE

"One of the best of the slam bang, hardboiled mystery adventure stories is this which deals with Rex McBride, a private detective assigned to find out who wants to wreck a big government dam project."

—*Chicago Daily Tribune*

"Intrigue, action, violence—excellent!"

—*The Cincinnati Enquirer*

"Thriller-mystery with a really new angle."

—*Los Angeles Times*

"It (*Sabotage*) is one of the best action detective stories you'll see in a long time. . . . Told with objectivity and not a spare word, this has a meaty plot, life-like characters and interesting settings."—*The San Diego Union*

Published by

E. P. DUTTON & CO., INC.

AND SUDDEN DEATH

CLEVE F. ADAMS

AND SUDDEN DEATH

NEW YORK
E. P. DUTTON & CO., INC.
1940

First Printing ....September 1940
Second Printing ....September 1940
Third Printing ....September 1940
Fourth Printing ....September 1940

This story appeared serially under the title "Homicide Honolulu Bound."

PRINTED IN THE UNITED STATES OF AMERICA
BY THE WILLIAM BYRD PRESS, INC.
RICHMOND, VIRGINIA

FOR
FRANCES

AND SUDDEN DEATH

AND SUDDEN DEATH, I

If McBride had not wanted to get out of town anyway he probably wouldn't have taken the job. Not that he didn't need the money; McBride usually needed money in large quantities. But chasing a woman over two or three thousand miles of Pacific Ocean in order to pay off a few odd gambling debts wouldn't have appealed to him except that he really did want to get away for a while.

Sheila Mason would be coming up for trial in a day or two now, and McBride, who had put her where she was, didn't want to be around. The taste of the last case was still bitter in his mouth, and he had a sickish, all-gone feeling in the pit of his stomach every time he read her name in print. He had been drinking more than was good for him.

He sat in an oddly ungraceful pose, humped over, hands between his spread knees, lean brown fingers drumming nervously on the edge of his chair. He was listening to Vickers with only half his mind. Late afternoon shadows licked at the tall windows of the office, blurred the blues and golds of the great Chinese rug, made of Vickers' pale face a blob of white behind the over-large, overly ornate desk. Vickers had taken off his glasses.

"You understand our position in this, McBride?"

"Sure," McBride said. "You're a glorified collection agency."

Vickers reached out and snapped on the desk lamp. The shadows fled. Vickers now became something more than just a shape in the semi-gloom. Iron-gray hair topped a bleakly austere face that was pale from lack of exposure to the sun, not from ill health. His gray eyes were curiously penetrating, even without the glasses. "I must say you don't appear very interested, Mr. McBride. Perhaps I've been misinformed. Possibly you are not the McBride recommended by the Underwriters' Alliance and practically every individual insurance company in California."

"I'm the guy," McBride said. He stood up. The act made him a personality, just as the light had Mr. Vickers. It wasn't that he was so tall; he was under six feet. But his well-tailored body gave the impression that it was all in one piece, built especially for him, not just a collection of odd parts taken at random from various assembly lines. Dark hair crowned a darkly good-looking face, sharply etched after the manner of the Sioux Indian. The eyes were perhaps the best key to his character. They reflected his capacity for deep, brooding silences, for sudden ribald laughter, for tremendous rages and an aloof arrogance bequeathed him by his Black Irish ancestors. He had come up from the gutter.

Vickers examined him with patent disfavor. "Please repeat what I have just told you, Mr. McBride. Short of an actual yawn you've done about everything to convince me of your complete boredom."

McBride's mouth was cynically humorous. "I'm sorry. It's just that I'm getting a little fed up with such terms as colossal, gigantic and stupendous. I was born in Hollywood, you see."

Vickers made a gesture eloquent of his utter disinterest in the circumstances of McBride's birth. "The matter under discussion, Mr. McBride, concerns two million dollars. By due process of law this money now belongs to the Monolith Corporation. We want it."

McBride decided to be unimpressed by two million dollars. "I've just finished a job involving a hundred million," he said. He moved over to the windows, pretending to be very interested in the rush of traffic below. Presently, realizing that he was acting like a sulky child, he turned. "All right, the crash of Southern Counties Building & Loan was the biggest thing in California history. Nordstrom wanted to be another Van Sweringen, or a Swedish match king or something. Others in the company had heads too big for their hats too. The crash and the subsequent investigation put three of these in Folsom for from two to ten years. Nordstrom himself got away clean. He had something over two million dollars in his pants at the time."

Vickers' eyes mirrored surprise. "I wouldn't have believed it. You actually heard me."

"Sure," McBride said. He grinned suddenly. "Forget it. It was just an act, same as yours. We all like to put it on for the boys once in a while."

Something that might have been a smile tugged at

the corners of the older man's mouth, but he carefully restrained himself to a brief clearing of the throat. He pointed his pince-nez at McBride's chest. "The receivers liquidated what they could. The Monolith Corporation bought up the balance, including the two millions Nordstrom absconded with. For three years we have had Nordstrom's wife under almost constant surveillance, hoping he would get in touch with her. At last it looks as though he has."

"What about the cops?"

Vickers permitted his mouth to droop a little. "The police files on the case are still open, though nothing has been done in that direction for over a year. My company thinks it advisable to go about the matter quietly, not informing the police, lest our flown bird again loses himself."

McBride laughed. "You talk as if you had him right in your hands."

"That will be your job," Vickers said. "To put Nels Nordstrom, or at least the two million, in our hands. The man himself is unimportant." He paused to clip the end from a cigar with meticulous care. "We do not know that Mrs. Nordstrom is attempting to join her husband. Our informant was unable to find that out."

"And who is your informant?"

"A maid," Vickers said. "A maid in the employ of the apartment house where Mrs. Nordstrom lives. She has supplied us with a great deal of data on the woman.

Our own staff has dug up more. We know, for instance, that Nordstrom, some time before the debacle, established a trust fund which pays Mrs. Nordstrom around five thousand a year. We were unable to touch the principal sum. But five thousand a year is less than pin money to Sybil Nordstrom." Vickers coughed slightly. "From the maid we understand that the lady in question has managed to eke out an existence through the acquaintanceship of various men about town."

McBride's eyes glowed. He had seen pictures of Sybil Nordstrom at the time of the crash. "Nice," he said softly. "Very nice indeed." He thought of something. "But if she's doing all right for herself here, why bother with her old man?"

"Two million dollars is a lot of money," Vickers pointed out. He watched McBride through narrowed eyes. "I understand you're quite a hand with the ladies."

McBride flushed. "Oh, so I'm to charm her into telling me where I can find her husband." He had not removed his topcoat. His hat, a fifteen-dollar Borsalino, lay on the desk. He picked this up and turned toward the door. "Well, it's been nice knowing you, Mr. Vickers."

Vickers stood up rather hurriedly. "Now wait a minute, McBride. I meant no offense. Your reputation is, of course, your own business. All we expect of you is results."

McBride paused with his hand on the knob. "No private dick in the world can guarantee you results. When you hire me—if you hire me—you can depend on it that I'll be in there trying. No more, no less." He took a slow breath. "Also, I'm nobody's pimp. I'd have to handle this in my own way."

"Of course," Vickers said. He sat down again. From a desk drawer he drew a thick Manila envelope. "The *Honolulu Queen* sails from San Pedro at two tomorrow. Mrs. Nordstrom will be on her. In this envelope is a first-class cabin reservation, together with ten thousand dollars. Whatever else you need is your own affair. We shall expect an accurate accounting of your expenditures."

"Meaning a swindle sheet?" McBride shook his head. "My God, what is this racket coming to?" He pointed a finger at Mr. Vickers. "Look, if there's any left I'll give it to you. If I need more I'll cable for it. Fair enough?"

Vickers opened his mouth, but no sound came out. Presently he closed it again and nodded an almost imperceptible affirmative. McBride was relieved. "I can't add up to ten thousand," he confided.

Vickers was not amused. "You may have a little competition, McBride. Our informant tells us there have been others inquiring about Mrs. Nordstrom's movements."

"Who, for instance?"

Vickers shrugged. "Who knows? Fenner? Teal?

Both were released around six months ago. O'Connor is still in. All of them have good reason to hate Nordstrom. He left them holding the sack. Also, and again, there is the little matter of two million dollars. Don't forget that."

"I won't," McBride promised. "I'll think of it as though it were my very own."

AND SUDDEN DEATH, II

THE city room of the *Tribune* was a hive of industry. McBride, who disliked hives of industry, and city rooms in particular, took a deep breath before letting the swing doors close behind him. He always felt that he was taking his life in his hands when he came up to see McGonigle, because even the copy boys acted like wild Indians around press time, and it was McBride's misfortune that never yet had he come up to see McGonigle when the presses weren't about to roll. McGonigle was on the desk. He was keeping a battery of phones hot, yelling at the rewrite men across from him, blue-penciling copy and trying to light a long-dead cigar all at the same time. The pneumatic tubes at his elbow kept plopping carriers into the basket, sucked the refills greedily down their brassy throats. McBride thought of the grimy men down in the bowels of the earth, like little devils shoveling coal into the fiery furnace of the presses. He was glad he did not work for a newspaper.

McGonigle scowled at him. "Oh, it's you again!"

McBride could not deny this. He bit the end from a fresh cigar, lit it, removed the stub of the old one from McGonigle's teeth and made the substitution. "Use your morgue a minute, pal?"

"What for?"

All of a sudden the din became terrific. McBride had

to raise his voice to a shout to make himself heard. "A bet!" he yelled. "I made a bet with a guy!"

"What kind of a bet?"

McBride clamped both hands over the pneumatics. "If I have to stay around here I'll even forget what it was about myself. Do I get an okay or don't I?"

McGonigle shoved the proof of an eight-column head across the desk. "Glad you dropped in, pal. You can give us a statement." The head screamed: "Sheila Mason turns State's evidence!" McBride could actually feel the blood drain from his face. Sheila had not only ratted on him, she was ratting on her pals. It's funny, he thought dully, funny I can still feel this way about her. It was as though someone had tied knots in his stomach. Presently he became aware that McGonigle was watching him. "No statement," he said in a curiously flat voice.

McGonigle tore the cigar to shreds. "Then the hell with you! No statement, no okay for the morgue. I'm tired doing you favors for nothing!"

McBride turned. "Okay, keed." Halfway down the city room something hit him in the small of the back. It was a brass carrier from the pneumatics. McGonigle was making frantic signals. McBride went back to the desk. "Well?"

McGonigle looked embarrassed. "Hell, Irish, you ought to know I didn't mean it." He gnawed at the knuckles of his left hand. With his right he wrote, "Investigator refuses comment." He shoved the sheet of gray copy paper at McBride. "Okay?"

"Okay," McBride said. He watched McGonigle scribble a pass to the morgue, accepted it without triumph. "Thanks, keed."

"The hell with you!" McGonigle shouted. He attacked a sheaf of AP stuff with a vicious pencil. McBride crossed the hall to the morgue. In here it was practically quiet. Around all four sides of the room and stacked in tiers down the center were steel files reaching clear to the ceiling, files which contained facts unprintable and otherwise about a great many people. A lanky kid with glasses came around one end of the center tier. McBride gave him McGonigle's note. He was trying desperately to think of a name close enough to Nordstrom to be in the same file. He finally decided on Nolan. "I'll take a look at the Nolan envelopes, Georgie. Don't bother to get 'em out. Just show me the drawer."

Georgie showed him the drawer. A ringing phone pulled him away for long enough for McBride to locate the Nordstrom folder and remove therefrom half-a-dozen glossy prints of pix taken prior to and during the three-year-old investigation. He was tucking these inside his coat, under an arm, when Georgie came back. Georgie looked at him suspiciously. "You take anything out, Mr. McBride?"

"Certainly not," McBride said with great dignity. "You think I'd do a thing like that, Georgie?" He had difficulty keeping the prints from slipping. "Why, Georgie, I'm surprised at you."

Georgie's pale eyes went to the raped folder. Mc-

Bride hadn't had time to get it all the way back and the exposed celluloid tab said Nordstrom as plain as day. McBride closed the drawer firmly. "Well, thanks a lot, pal." He went out to the hall and stood in front of the elevator bank. He was still standing there when McGonigle came barging out of the city room. "Hey, you!"

McBride turned with an affectation of pleased surprise. "Why, hello there, pal. You get the baby to bed?"

McGonigle was practically foaming at the mouth. "I might have known it! Nurse a viper to your bosom and that's what you get."

McBride was outraged. "Who's a viper?"

"You are, you big heel! What were you doing in the Nordstrom file."

"Nordstrom?" McBride's brows drew down in a pretense of great concentration. "Why, I don't know what you mean, pal. Who says I was in the Nordstrom file?"

"Georgie says so!" McGonigle yelled. He tore his hair in an access of rage. "I might have known it!"

McBride laid calming hands on the smaller man's shoulders. This was a difficult feat, because he had to keep his right elbow tight against his body. "Now look, Pete, I accidentally yanked a folder out of the file. Come to think of it, I guess the name might have been Nordstrom at that. But I was looking for a guy named Pinky Nolan—used to be a pork-and-beaner out at the Legion Stadium. Would I be looking in the

Nordstrom file for a guy named Nolan? I can read, can't I?"

"So can I!" McGonigle yelled. "I can even read between the lines. You're working on a kill that might just happen to involve Sybil Nordstrom, and you come up here and give me a song and dance about ——" He ran out of breath.

McBride wet his lips. So there had been a kill, had there? A kill in what had promised to be nothing more than an interesting chase after a couple of million dollars. He tried to make his voice casual, realized instantly that he couldn't do it and resorted to violent anger. "So you spied on me, did you? You give me a courtesy pass to your lousy morgue and then you call the kid and tell him to see what I'm after." He waved a hand. "Oh, don't bother to deny it. I heard the phone!"

McGonigle's mouth fell open. "Well, now look, Rex——"

"A fine business!" McBride shouted. "A fine business, I must say, spying on your best friends." He and McGonigle had quite an audience by now. Half of the city room was out in the corridor, and a couple of elevator boys were arguing with the kid from the morgue. Georgie looked a little frightened and McBride took instant advantage of this. "Look at him!" he directed McGonigle. "Ask him to his face if he actually saw me in the Nordstrom file." His voice became tinged with sorrow. "Why, Georgie!"

"Well," Georgie said doubtfully, "well——"

"You see?" McBride said plaintively. He let his shoulders droop. "I've been accused of a lot of things, but never anything like this." Righteous anger gripped him anew. "What is all this about a kill, anyway? And who is Sybil Nordstrom?"

McGonigle by this time was almost in tears. "Hell, Rex, no use getting sore. I'm supposed to be a newspaper man and you're usually good for news. So I did call the kid. I admit it." He spread his hands. "And then when he said you'd had the Nordstrom file out—well, coincidence is a funny thing but I didn't think it was that funny."

"You're still talking Greek," McBride said. He appealed to the gallery. "Isn't he talking Greek?"

McGonigle glared at his minions. "Come on, gang, break it up. We're supposed to be getting out a paper." He took McBride's arm in a gesture of loving faith. "Nothing to it, I guess. Some maid out at the Chelsea Arms just got knocked off. I understood Sybil Nordstrom was still living there, and then when you—I mean, when I *thought* you——"

"I get it," McBride said. He bent a forgiving eye on McGonigle. "Forget it, old pal, old pal." Entering one of the waiting elevators he tripped and almost lost the pictures. The last he saw of his old pal, McGonigle's face was getting all ready to be suspicious again. The elevator dropped to street level. McBride went into the nearest bar and had two quick ones. He needed them.

Presently he caught a cab and went home. This was a bungalow court in Hollywood, just off the Boulevard, and it had the most amazingly active fountain in the whole world. The court itself was mediocre, the usual double row of pseudo-Spanish stucco-and-tile units separated by lawn and a flagged patio. But the fountain, especially at night, was a glory to behold. Neon-tinted jets of spray liberally besprinkled the unwary passer-by, and it was thought great fun by many of the tenants to dunk their guests in the lily pond at the fountain's base. McBride liked the place because nobody, not even the management, minded what you did or when you did it. The cops always had a tough time finding out who started the fight.

McBride let himself into the fifth unit on the left, snapped on the lights, went through the living room to the kitchen where he poured himself another stiffish drink. The death of the maid was beginning to get to him now. He wondered if Sybil Nordstrom had killed her. He did not, at the moment, consider himself in any imminent danger, though there was always the possibility that McGonigle would discover the loss of the prints and tip off the police. And the cops, in turn, might think it even more of a coincidence than McGonigle had. If Sybil Nordstrom had done the job, and had been just a little careless about it, McBride's interest in the Nordstrom file could easily be construed as part and parcel of the kill itself. While McGonigle was a dearly beloved pal, McBride wouldn't have trusted him any farther than he could throw a bull by the tail.

Presently he went back into the living room and

surveyed the pile of luggage in the middle of the floor. He wasn't at all sure that he was going to need it now. It was quite possible that Sybil Nordstrom wasn't going any place more distant than the Hall of Justice. The telephone rang. McBride waited till it had rung three times before answering it. Finally, though, he could stand the suspense no longer. It turned out to be Vickers calling.

Vickers was agitated. "Have you heard the news, McBride?"

"What news?" McBride asked cautiously.

"About the maid, of course."

"Oh, that."

"My God," Vickers jittered, "I must say you don't seem to take it very seriously!"

"Why should I?" McBride demanded. "I didn't even know it was the right maid. But if you say so——"

Vickers mastered his emotion with difficulty. You could actually hear him mastering it. "See here, McBride, we don't know that Sybil Nordstrom——"

"Killed her?"

"Don't say it!" Vickers gasped. "Don't even breathe it. If it were known that we—I mean if the police were to find out that this girl was actually in our employ, that we had information we hadn't passed on"—he drew a ragged breath—"Well, the Monolith Corporation can't afford to be mixed up in any scandal."

McBride's mouth was cynical. "Of course not. No, the thing to do it just let a girl be murdered and forget the whole business. She was watching Sybil Nordstrom for you, but the police needn't know that, need they?"

"McBride, I give you my word that if I was sure the Nordstrom woman had done it I'd turn her in immediately." His voice became plaintive. "But how can we be sure? There are too many angles to this affair."

McBride whistled through his teeth. "What have the police done on it so far?"

"Not a thing except establish the caliber of the weapon. It was a thirty-two. No motive."

"I like that," McBride said. "No motive."

"Well, you asked what the police had discovered. I told you."

"Have they questioned Mrs. Nordstrom?"

"Only as one of the tenants. I tell you, McBride, we can not be sure she did it. A girl like that—the maid, I mean—a girl who is willing to sell information could be mixed up in any one of a hundred things." Vickers put a lot of sincerity into his next words: "But if you have any scruples, why not follow the woman as we planned, find out definitely whether she did or did not do the—ah—deed?"

McBride's eyes smoldered. "And if I find out she did?"

"Perhaps you won't until after you find the—ah—"

"Two million?"

Vickers lost his temper. "Damn it all, McBride, I don't like your implications."

"Nor I yours," McBride said shortly. He hung up on this note of mutual hostility.

AND SUDDEN DEATH, III

Miss Ford, whom McBride had fully expected to hang, or at least send up to San Quentin instead of Sheila Mason, was unusually lovely in a green and gold creation which she could not possibly have bought on a secretary's salary. This was a source of annoyance to McBride, who fancied himself a pretty fair dick, as detectives go. She had been a secretary when he met her; she was still a secretary. How she managed to dress as she did, and to support an apartment the like of which you saw only in the movies, remained a deep dark mystery. In response to McBride's thinly veiled allusions to women who were not quite nice she sometimes spoke of a rich uncle. McBride had never met the uncle.

The Cocoanut Grove was literally crawling with celebrities tonight. It was the supper hour, just before midnight, and there must have been a world première some place, because Hollywood was there in all its magnificence. Under the swaying fronds of the palms, genuine, and the blue of the starry sky, artificial, a billion dollars worth of talent ate and drank and danced and sparred for the limelight. Miss Ford, more worthy of note than any of the female contingent, appeared quite content with McBride. She had the darkest blue eyes he had ever seen, and her hair, done high on her head tonight, was so dark it seemed to hold bluish shadows. The perfume of it almost drove him wild at times.

"You're beautiful," he said. This was perhaps the tenth time he had said it in the last hour. He drank thirstily of his champagne. "Beautiful."

She leaned toward him. "So you're going away."

Her eyes made him vaguely uncomfortable. "Unh-hunh." He refilled her glass, then his own. "Little job in Chicago."

"Perhaps I should have said running away."

He laughed. "From what?"

"From yourself, I think."

Quite suddenly he knew this to be true. At the back of his mind had been the thought that he would not stop at Honolulu; that no matter what developed in the Nordstrom case he would just keep on going, on and on, indefinitely, until time or distance or something should ease this aching hurt that was in him. And now Miss Ford, in a couple of words, had shown him how futile it all would be. He half rose. "I think we had better be going," he said roughly.

She put out a hand, detaining him. "Sit down a moment, Rex. You are angry with me. I don't want you to go away being—angry."

Something, some little inflection of her voice, told him that he wasn't fooling her a bit. She knew he was running out on her too, not for just a few days, but for good. And she was taking it like a soldier. Her eyes were almost violet now. The music from the orchestra shell nagged at him. "I am not angry with you," he said irritably. "It's just that——"

She nodded. "I know, Rex." Her smile was faintly cynical. "You see, it happens that I feel about you the way you think you feel about—her."

He was definitely angry now. "Leave her out of it."

"I can't," she said quietly. "Not and discuss you."

He made a bitter mouth. "You don't have to discuss me. I'm a heel. I admit it. What else is there to discuss?" Suddenly the full meaning of her previous words struck him. "What do you mean, the way I *think* I feel?"

Miss Ford examined the palm of her hand. "You don't really love her, Rex. You never did. She was just something that you couldn't get and, you being you, it was a sort of challenge. You wouldn't have turned her in if you'd really loved her."

"The hell I wouldn't!"

"No," Miss Ford said, "you wouldn't have. People just aren't built that way." She shrugged a thought away. "Once in a blue moon, Rex, a man is born who might consider his job, his integrity, of greater importance than the woman he loves. You are not that man. You may like to think you are, because you are a supreme egoist." Her fine eyes grew a little misty, but her mouth still smiled. "You see, I know you better than you know yourself."

He laughed harshly. "Thanks for nothing."

She stood up. "All right, Rex. I just wanted to give

you something to think about while you are in—Chicago, wasn't it?"

He flushed hotly. "Damn it all, Kay, if you think I'm lying to you, why do you bother with me?"

She didn't answer that one. He held her cloak for her. "Well?"

"Think it over, Rex. You are just sore. Someone you trusted fooled you. It's your ego that is wounded, not your heart." She looked him full in the face. "Well, *bon voyage*."

He was startled. "Why do you say it that way?"

She picked up her bag. "I stopped by your place earlier this evening. Your luggage seemed a little elaborate for, shall we say, Chicago?"

His eyes were suddenly ashamed. "You're rather a grand guy, Kay. Maybe part of what you say is true. Maybe—" He broke off to stare unseeingly across the crowded supper room. "But hell, I've got to find out for myself, haven't I?" He shrugged. "Besides, I've got a job to do."

"Of course."

He laid a bill on the table and they moved up the aisle toward the check room. A man came through the swinging glass doors of the cocktail lounge. He was very drunk. McBride, recognizing this fact without identifying the man himself, attempted to push on past and was suddenly clutched in a fond embrace.

"Good ol' McBride," the man giggled. "Good ol' McBride." He peered cunningly up at McBride's angry face. "Been lookin' all over for you, McBride."

McBride cursed him. "Scram, sucker."

"Not me," the drunk snickered. "You're the sucker, not me." He laid a waggish finger alongside his nose. "Ol' Man wantsa see you. Wantsa see you private and in terrific hurry."

McBride really looked at the guy this time. Vaguely he remembered seeing him around the press room at Headquarters. Obviously the guy was a legman for one of the papers and McBride didn't need three guesses to pick the *Tribune* as the right one. The Old Man mentioned could be none other than McGonigle. The two-timing rat had discovered the loss of the pix. McBride scowled. "You tell McGonigle to go to hell."

"Not me, pal, not me. Tell him yourself." One eye closed in a prodigious wink. "Ol' man gimme a message." He giggled. "S'like a password, kind of." He now closed both eyes, repeating from memory. "Ol' Man says, 'You tell that bastard McBride "Honolulu." ' Jussa one word, see? 'Honolulu.' "

"Okay, okay," McBride snarled. He turned harried eyes on Kay Ford. "Come on, hon, let's get out of here before I start foaming at the mouth." They left the legman teetering on his heels and staring stupidly after them. Getting his coat and hat at the check room McBride carefully avoided Kay's eyes. "It's just a gag," he muttered. "Just a gag, hon. That crazy McGonigle likes his little joke."

"I understand, Rex." Her face was almost as white as her ermine cloak. They went out the side door to the parking area and McBride put her in a cab. "Mind if I don't take you home, Kay? I've got to see this heel in kind of a hurry."

She put out a gloved hand. "Then this is good-by, Rex?"

There was no use keeping up the pretense any longer. Even if she hadn't already guessed, that stumble-bum of a reporter would have clinched it with his bibulous repetition of McGonigle's one-word message. McBride, cornered, could meet a problem as squarely as anybody. He put a hand under her chin. "We've had a lot of good times together, kitten. You've been swell. But I don't think I'm doing you any good, and maybe there's someone else around who will. I'm shoving off." He bent forward to kiss her for the last time.

She pushed him away. "Good-by, Rex."

The cab door slammed and then she was gone. He stood there a moment, head bared, watching the cab whirl down the long ramp, watching the taillight merge with the thousand other taillights on Wilshire Boulevard. Presently he turned and went back into the hotel and found a phone booth.

McGonigle's voice was smooth as castor oil. "Hello, there, old pal, old pal. I knew I could depend on you."

"Don't pal me, you Irish blackguard! What's the idea sending a lush after me with some kind of a screwy message about Honolulu?"

McGonigle was horified. "Was he really lushed?"

"Stinko."

McGonigle thought this was very funny. "Hah-hah-

hah. Well, with a reputation like yours, what did you expect? He probably looked in all the bars first."

McBride sucked in his breath. "You haven't answered my question."

"Haven't I?" McGonigle purred. McBride could almost see him licking his fat lips. "Well, then, I will. Listen carefully, my sweet and scented thief. You copped some pix from our files. To be more specific, from the Nordstrom file. Prior to this a maid was found murdered in her room in the Nordstrom apartment house. Curiously enough, this maid had from time to time been in attendance on Sybil Nordstrom. Am I making myself clear?"

"Not to me you're not. If you think I stole some pix why don't you swear out a warrant?"

"Now Rex, would I do that to a pal?" McGonigle almost wept. "Besides," he added presently, "I don't give one little damn about the pictures. I haven't even bothered to look for them. You may keep them as a slight token of the *Tribune's* gratitude for what you are about to do."

"Oh, so I'm about to do something, am I?"

McGonigle's voice lost its purr. "You're damned right you are. And you'd better do a good job too, or we'll throw you in the can so fast it'll make your head swim!"

"Listen," McBride yelled, "listen to me, you baboon, don't go throwing your weight around or I'll come up there and take you apart with my two hands!"

McGonigle made derisive sounds. "There are two

dicks just around the corner. I told them I might have a story for them."

"Am I scared!"

"Well," McGonigle said, "maybe you're not, at that. Maybe you're even a bigger fool than I think you are, though that hardly seems possible." He lowered his voice. "Look, with the murder of the maid, and the stolen pix of the Nordstrom clan; with the lovely Sybil off to Honolulu to meet, no doubt, a gent with two million stolen dollars; with the well-known private investigator Rex McBride sailing on the same ship—" McGonigle broke off to chuckle nastily. "I ask you, wouldn't that make a pretty dish to set before the cops? Here's an eight-column head I just thought up: 'Detective Arrested as Accessory in Mystery Slaying!' "

"How do I know who killed the maid?" McBride yelled. "Let the cops hold her if they've got anything on her!"

"Struggle, little fly," McGonigle cooed. "The cops are stymied for want of a motive. They, as yet, do not know that the lovely Sybil is going to the isles of enchantment. Nor do they know that you are. They do not run a newspaper, you see, so little things like sailings and passenger lists do not always come within their ken." His voice lost its bantering note. "Listen, McBride, you don't even have to tell me who you're working for. My guess is the Monolith Corporation. Now you either do what I want you to do, or I'll hand the cops the yarn. Monolith, and you as its employee, found out, presumably through the maid, that Sybil Nordstrom was on her way. Did you tell the cops? No, you were afraid they'd bungle the job and your two million would get away from you again. By God, you're even willing to condone a murder in order to recover a little filthy lucre!"

"But *you're* not!" McBride sneered. "What the hell are you talking to me for? You've got it all. Go ahead and call copper."

McGonigle tossed the bludgeon overboard. He became slyly insinuating. "But perhaps I have misjudged you, my boy. Perhaps I've even misjudged Mrs. Nordstrom. Maybe she didn't kill the maid because the maid happened to know something Mrs. Nordstrom didn't want known." He sighed. "Possibly you yourself are not fully convinced of her guilt. You are following her for, among other things, of course, additional proof. Isn't this true?"

"You sound like Vickers," McBride said. "Both of you leave a nasty taste in my mouth. What is it you want?"

"It occurs to me that there is an even greater story in prospect than the one we have now." McGonigle sighed pleasurably. "How I wish I were going with you. The dauntless, untiring chase of a beautiful woman over the seven seas. The treasure at last. Victory. And an exclusive for the *Los Angeles Tribune*."

"So that's it," McBride said. "I didn't think there was anything lower than a private dick, but I guess there is."

"Well, suit yourself, McBride. If she killed that maid she ought to hang. If she didn't, the motive we could furnish her would be enough to hold her here indefinitely. Bang would go your chance at the two million, because it's a cinch Nordstrom would hear and be on his way again. Not that you and Monolith would be worrying about that. You'd be in the coop facing a conspiracy charge."

McBride knew this to be a fact. McGonigle had nothing to lose. He would get a story either way. On the whole he was relieved at McGonigle's request, because it really entailed no additional effort on his, McBride's, part. The only catch seemed to be that with so many other actors on the scene it was going to be a little difficult to deliver an exclusive. He mentioned this to McGonigle.

"You'd better," McGonigle said grimly. "You'd better deliver, or else. We could just as easily pretend that we didn't learn about the missing pix and one thing and another till after you'd sailed. Cross us up and your heinie will be in a sling no matter where you are."

"A fine thing!" McBride said bitterly. He hurled the unforgivable epithet at the mouthpiece, banged the receiver down and slammed out of the booth. Presently he was in a cab and on the way across La Brea toward home. He tried not to think about Kay Ford, but it was no good. Somehow, with all the things in the world to think about, her white face kept popping up in front of him, not accusing exactly, but disillusioned and tinged faintly with something that might have been disgust. McBride didn't blame her. He was more than a little disgusted with himself.

It was just 12:30 when the cab drew up before the court. Paying off the hacker, McBride looked along the flagged walk to where the most magnificent fountain in Hollywood lay in wait for the unwary. He was, he thought gloomily, going to miss that fountain. Like a beacon it had guided him to the right door on many a night. He went up the walk, skirting the fountain cagily, so that only one side of him got wet. There were three or four hilarious parties going on in adjacent bungalows, and the light from several open windows showed him that his own shades were drawn. They hadn't been drawn when he left. He stood there a moment, key ready, listening. Aside from the noise of the parties he could make out no other sound. No one seemed to be moving inside; certainly there were no lights.

Finally he thrust the key home, flung the door inward; then, side-stepping, he reached in and snapped the wall switch. Nothing happened. McBride didn't know what he had expected to happen, but he was positive that someone other than he had pulled the blinds. Presently, convinced that there were no lurking assassins beyond the portal, he went in. Someone had very thoroughly ransacked, not only his luggage, but the entire three rooms and bath.

Instantly his mind leaped to McGonigle, then to the police, but after the first heat of his rage had passed he saw that neither suspicion was exactly justified. The cops would want him, McBride, not any of his possessions. And McGonigle had said he hadn't even bothered to look for the pictures. As a matter of fact, the pictures were still propped up on the mantle, where McBride had been studying them. Too, McGonigle had had all the information he needed without this.

A quick check-up showed nothing whatever to be missing, and this alone made the possibility of a chance prowler ridiculous. McBride's guns would have brought a hundred dollars in any hock shop on Main Street, his studs and spare watch another five or six. They were still where he had left them. He shivered a little, because it is one thing to know what you're up against, another to be stumbling around in the dark. What had promised to be a comparatively secret mission was rapidly turning into something like a three-ring circus.

McBride went over and stood in front of the likeness of Sybil Nordstrom. "Baby," he said, "you're certainly causing me a lot of trouble."

AND SUDDEN DEATH, IV

SHE was a good boat, the *Honolulu Queen.* Of something under 20,000 tons and with an overall length of less than 700 feet she was by no means as big as the *Queen Mary* or the *Normandie.* But she had something, an intangible something, that they did not have. She was a live, sentient thing, a glistening white greyhound, lying there in her berth, panting a little, eager for the long run across the Pacific. McBride's heart swelled a little with pride, because it now seemed that the United States was getting a few bottoms of her own.

He was up on A deck, at the inshore rail, studying the crowd far below through a pair of binoculars. Vickers had said there might be some competition in this chase, and after last night McBride was ready to believe him. He still was without a motive for the search of his rooms.

Around and about him was the bustle of imminent departure. Seven hundred passengers take a lot of handling, and their shore-going friends do little to simplify matters. Stewards, deck officers, palpitant old ladies and seasoned travelers jostled McBride as if he were just another rail stanchion. A stiff breeze ruffled the channel, and the bright afternoon sun was reflected on the waters in a million pinpoints of light. Sailing time was just fifteen minutes away.

McBride had already seen Sybil Nordstrom to her cabin. She had a lanai suite on A deck. A little late himself, he had been unable to check last-minute additions to the printed passenger lists, and anyway it was quite likely that the men he was looking for would be using assumed names. Following Mrs. Nordstrom they would not want her to know they were aboard. McBride, fortified with excellent, though stolen, photographs of both Saul Fenner and George Teal, was not dependent on names. They could call themselves Mike and Ike for all he cared. He wondered a little about Frank O'Connor, the O'Connor who was still in Folsom. There was something about this third man of the sentenced trio that he felt he should remember. It wasn't that O'Connor had continued to protest his innocence in the face of overwhelming evidence to the contrary; it was something else, some vague bit of information that the papers hadn't made much over at the time, but that had appealed to McBride. He, of course, had not been on the case. What interest he had taken had been solely as a reader of the news. And now, after three years, it was difficult to remember even some of the important angles. All he was sure of, all anyone was sure of, was that Nels Nordstrom had vanished into thin air. McBride hoped Nordstrom was a frugal man; that he hadn't spent the two million.

And here again was the tremendous gamble that the gorgeous Sybil wasn't on the way to meet her old man at all. Maybe she was just taking herself a ride. Being as discreet as possible McBride had ascertained that she wasn't accompanied by anyone; at least not openly. This seemed to indicate that she did intend to meet her husband. Also, there was the matter of the murdered maid and the search of McBride's effects. He was by no means sure that Mrs. Nordstrom was directly responsible for either of these acts. As a matter of fact he had practically absolved her of the killing, because a .32 is hardly a woman's weapon. The police had definitely established the caliber of the lethal bullet. But it was almost a foregone conclusion that both jobs, coming so closely on the heels of the information that Sybil was going bye-bye, were in some way connected with the fact itself. McBride sighed. His only source of satisfaction so far lay in the fact that he had ten grand of the Monolith Corporation's money. He wondered if they let you shoot craps aboard the *Honolulu Queen*. He was not much of a hand for bridge.

The second warning whistle had blown, and McBride was still peering downward through his glasses when he felt a hand on his arm. "Pardon me, may I borrow those a moment?"

McBride turned. The hand and the cultured voice belonged to a Japanese, a very special sort of Japanese, the kind you would expect to find on the A deck of a liner like the *Queen*. He was small, slender, excellently turned out. His skin was lighter than McBride's own and there was no flatness to the face, scarcely any slant to the eyes. Also, and this pleased McBride most, the little man was not obsequious.

"Someone I am expecting," he said.

"He'll have to hurry, then," McBride smiled. He passed over the binoculars. The little man thanked him, turned his attention on the crowd below. They were already closing the after gangway. A single tug puffed noisily against the pull of the bow hawser. The *Queen* lay headed into the channel and all that was necessary was to get her far enough out of the slip to give her steerage. McBride had seen many a ship go down the San Pedro channel under her own power. He had never been on one. He expected to be very sick indeed after a while.

The Japanese turned from the rail. "Thank you," he said gravely. "Thank you very much. My friend will not come now."

McBride accepted the glasses. "Tough," he said.

The little man's mustache made a shallow V when he smiled. "It is of no importance." He put out a small, well-cared-for hand. "May I present myself? I am the Baron Ito Itsuki, attached to the Japanese consulate at Los Angeles."

McBride shook the hand enthusiastically. This was not all pretense. He really liked the little guy's looks. "McBride," he said. "Rex McBride. Not attached to anything." He grinned. "You wouldn't be a crap-shooter, would you, Baron?"

Itsuki said he had been known to indulge. It developed that in his younger days he had graduated from Stanford. McBride was impressed. He had never gotten beyond the eighth grade, himself. They talked of this and that while the *Honolulu Queen* was being warped into mid-channel. Up on the boat deck an orchestra played the "Song of the Islands," and people cheered and flags waved and it was quite an occasion. A little lump came into McBride's throat, because he and Sheila Mason had once talked of making a trip like this together. One of her favorite melodies, he remembered, was "Sweet Leilani." He hoped he would never hear it again.

Itsuki crinkled his eyes against the sun. "A great country, yours." He removed his hat.

Almost unconsciously McBride did the same. They stood there like that, watching Pedro dwindle in the distance, and finally the great gray ships of the Pacific Fleet in the outer harbor. Presently McBride asked the inevitable question. "Vacation?"

Itsuki shrugged. "I am on my way to Yokohama. After that, who knows?" He gave McBride one of his quick, friendly smiles. "I will see you later, perhaps?"

"Sure." McBride watched the little man make his way with unhurried dignity toward the lanai suites up forward. He envied Itsuki his tailor and his vast calm. He wished more people could know that all Japanese did not hiss politely when they spoke, and say, "So sorry," at least twice during every observation. He wished he had a drink, but instead of going to the nearest bar and getting one he descended, via the after elevator, to B deck and Number 47, his own cabin.

Presently, shorn of his coat and flat on his back on the divan, he again held communion with the half-dozen glossy prints he had stolen from the *Tribune's* files. He was beginning to feel that he had known the subjects always; that, in a way, they were all just having a friendly little game of strip poker.

There was Saul Fenner, for instance. McBride regarded Fenner's likeness with an unprejudiced eye. At the time the picture was taken, presumably during the trial, Fenner had been an enormously fat man. He might have lost some of that as a guest of the state. McBride had heard they didn't feed you so good at Folsom. Fenner looked a great deal like Roscoe Arbuckle, only he wore pince-nez and his thinning hair was parted in the center. He didn't look like a particularly vengeful man. Avaricious perhaps, possibly dangerous if sufficiently aroused, but not the type to court physical violence.

McBride discarded Soul Fenner and took up Mr. George Teal. Now there was a guy it would pay to watch. Mr. Teal was tall and thin and dark. His mouth said he was dyspeptic. There were two pictures of Mr. Teal, because of the three indicted Nordstrom associates he was considered the most important. He had been the first vice-president of the scuttled corporation. McBride did not know why Teal and Fenner should have been released from prison before the comparatively obscure O'Connor, who was only the treasurer. Maybe O'Connor had a legitimate beef at that. Maybe they had all ganged up on him.

McBride scowled at the saturnine Mr. Teal. "You are a rat," he said. "Even if you're reformed and are not aboard this boat, I still think you are a rat." Perhaps his judgment was influenced a trifle by the subtle rise and fall of the *Honolulu Queen*, which was now breasting the long swells of the open sea. He was not as yet sick, but he fully expected to be. That is why he was lying down, prepared for it, as for an operation.

McBride laid Mr. Teal face down on the bed and, saving the Nordstroms for the last, like dessert, examined Frank O'Connor. On the whole, he was glad that Frank O'Connor was still in prison, because if he, McBride, were at any time likely to be caught in the middle he would just as soon not have this man O'Connor as one of the converging forces. It wasn't that he was so big, or that he exuded ferocity. Neither was he a young man. McBride placed him as somewhere in his fifties. Hair that probably had once been red was now white, and there were vertical lines at the corners of the mouth, as though the man were accustomed to rigid self-repression. The eyes were either a gray or a light blue, and they looked straight at you, clear and unafraid. McBride figured the O'Connor for a good hater. Again something nagged at his memory, some little thing about O'Connor that he should know. It still wouldn't jell.

He tackled Nels Nordstrom next. Here was the dominant personality of the lot; the man who had sold Southern Counties Building and Loan to the whole of California, and finally sold it down the river. Except for want of a beard he might have posed as the legendary Viking of old. A great golden man with a blonde mane and piercing eyes, he was surprisingly young to have conceived and carried out so gigantic a swindle. He had been an All-American tackle. McBride said, "Boy, if you're still around you shouldn't be hard to find."

Nordstrom's eyes seemed to say, "Then find me, McBride. Come on and find me."

McBride flung the picture from him. "Nels, old pal, you don't know the half of it. I've got your wife." He smacked his lips over the luscious Sybil. "Maybe I'll take you on at that, baby." He suddenly thought of what Vickers had suggested and hurled the luscious Sybil across the cabin. "Nuts, I'm through with women!"

He sat up as someone knocked on the door. "Come in!"

It turned out to be his steward. He was a smallish man with sandy hair and eyes like a spaniel's. "Help you unpack, sir?"

"Sure," McBride said. "You don't even have to help. You can do all of it."

"Thank you, sir." He went busily to work. When he came to McBride's two guns he paused, hefting them. His manner was only mildly curious. "Are you a gangster, sir?"

"Sure," McBride said. "I'm Capone. I just had my face lifted." He grinned engagingly. "What's your name, pal?"

The steward put the guns down on the dresser. "Simmons, sir."

McBride stood up, yawning. "Then remember this, Simmons, don't tell anybody who I really am and maybe we'll both be alive when we make Honolulu. You'd like that, wouldn't you?"

Simmons shivered. "Oh, quite, Mr. McBride." He finished stowing McBride's gear rather hurriedly. McBride, opening one of the portholes, sucked great draughts of salt air into his lungs. He was surprised to find that he wasn't sick at all. In a way this was a disappointment, because he was one who liked to have his expectations realized.

Simmons, returning from the luggage room across the passage, inquired if there would be anything else. McBride said there wouldn't. "Thank you, sir," Simmons said. "Just ring if you want me, sir." He saluted briskly. McBride felt nautical as hell. Presently he donned a tweed sports coat instead of the suit coat he had discarded, tugged a cap down on his head and went out to the passage, intending to take a hike along the promenade. Locking his door he became conscious of a woman just turning away from Cabin 49, two doors down. Her back was toward him, but there was something familiar about that back. The slim length of her, the way she carried her head set up a tremendous hammering in his chest. He strode forward, caught her arm roughly. "Well, for Christ's sake, what are you doing here?"

"Hello, Rex," Miss Ford said.

AND SUDDEN DEATH, V

"I WON'T have it!" McBride shouted. "You can't do this to me!" He was perfectly safe in shouting, because he and Kay Ford apparently had the boat deck to themselves. Forward, the officers' quarters and all of the bridge but the wing tips were screened from view by the gymnasium and the medicinal baths. The tennis courts were deserted. Towering above them the giant funnels belched a scarcely discernible blue haze, yet the *Queen* was turning up her advertised twenty-two knots. A stiff offshore breeze blew the tops off the moderately tall seas and made a rainbow-hued fog of the spray above the churning wake. Downdraft tugged playfully at Miss Ford's skirts.

"You won't have what, Rex?" Her blue eyes laughed at him. "Who was it that practically knocked me down in the corridor and dragged me up here?"

"It isn't decent!" he yelled. "Chasing a man all over the Pacific Ocean—it isn't decent, I tell you!"

She dropped her eyes demurely. "Why, Rex McBride, how can you say such a thing? You know very well you told me you were going to Chicago."

He scowled. "And I also told you I was shoving off, pulling my freight, that I was all through." He pointed a finger at her. "And anyway, don't give me that old stuff. You knew damned well I was lying, even before that lush reporter laid an egg." He drew a deep breath, expelled it with a tremendous whooshing sound. "Christ!"

She looked at him. "Are you working on something, Rex, or is it just—the other thing?"

He had the grace to flush under her calm scrutiny. "I am working. I've got a screw-ball of a case, but I've got plenty of time to think too. Nothing much can happen for the four days we're aboard." He glared at her. "But hell's fire, how can a guy think when you're around?"

She stared off at the horizon. "I won't bother you, Rex."

"Then what the hell did you come along for?"

"I don't know," she said dully. "Just the ride, I guess." Presently she turned and went toward one of the after companions leading below. He stared after her with sultry eyes. "Beautiful," he thought. "Beautiful and smart, and I haven't got the sense that God gave dumb animals."

For a little while he stood there at the starboard rail, eyes on the limitless sea, mind turned inward upon himself. A curious combination of introvert and extrovert, which should have made him a normal man, he had these periods of self-analysis in which he was able to project his own personality against the screen of circumstance and examine it with absolute honesty. At times like these he was not very proud of what he found. He was, he thought, an over-sexed egoist whose infrequent impulses toward decency frequently came to naught. Such honor as he had was flavored with the guttersnipe cynicism of the city-bred kid who lives and breathes and eventually survives by virtue of his own two fists. The veneer of civilization he had acquired, the thing that made him acceptable in all walks of life, was only a cloak, and he knew it. When he thought of God, as he sometimes did, he thought that God must be having a lot of fun watching the conflict of emotions which was Rex McBride.

Presently, shrugging, he spat disgustedly over the rail, as though by so doing he could rid himself of the bitter taste in his mouth, and went below. Purely by accident he found himself in the men's club room, a strictly stag apartment, and here for the first time he was able to examine the last-minute revisions appended to the passenger list. There was no one named Fenner, none named Teal. Sybil Nordstrom's name appeared on the regular list. Apparently she had made her reservation some time in advance. Again it was the merest accident that McBride's index finger, pausing briefly beside the Nordstrom entry, should move on down to the O's. There were three O'Connors aboard, none of them Franks. The thing that caused McBride to suck in his breath sharply was the unusual Christian name of the third O'Connor. It was Chalice, and this was the thing that had eluded McBride's groping memory. Frank O'Connor, who was now residing in a California penitentiary, had had a daughter. Her name was Chalice, and McBride's musical ear had caught and retained the sound of it long after the case itself was forgotten. So Chalice O'Connor is among those present, he thought. I wonder if she is as good a hater as her father.

He made a mental note of her cabin number, a first-class suite on B deck not so very far from his own. It was odd, he thought, that she should use her own name. It was almost certain that Sybil Nordstrom would see it. But perhaps the gorgeous Sybil had not known of the girl Chalice in the heyday of the Nordstrom rise to fame and fortune. The girl herself had not been subpoenaed during the trial. She had been merely a name, dragged in once or twice along toward the end. On the other hand, it was possible Sybil Nordstrom was meant to see and recognize the name. While this was not likely, it was nonetheless a possibility. McBride filed the item away at the back of his mind and went into the adjacent bar.

There was quite a little crowd in here. The room was paneled in a dozen different woods, carpeted with a deep-piled tweed broadloom. The tables were leather-topped, the chairs leather and dark oak, studded with copper nails. It was typically a man's room and McBride relaxed gratefully. Not even Kay Ford could get to him in here. He sat on a tall stool at the bar and ordered a rye Collins. This was the first drink he had had all day. He sipped it with the virtuous complacency of a man who has proved beyond the shadow of a doubt that he is his own master. The talk around and about him was of the coming election. He did not join in the discussion. When asked his opinion by the bibulous young man on the next stool he merely shook his head sadly, giving the impression that he viewed the outlook with alarm. Presently he got up and went over to where, above the fireplace, was a framed deck plan of the *Honolulu Queen*, done in colors and with cabalistic symbols to differentiate the toilets from the wardrobes.

Except for the scarcely perceptible rise and fall of the floor under him there was no sensation of twenty-thousand-odd tons of steel plowing its way through endless gray-green seas. He might have been in any one of a dozen Hollywood hotels. It was growing dark outside now, and a little chill. A steward came in and lighted the fire.

McBride spoke to him. "I'm green at this business. Do we dress for dinner tonight?"

"That's optional with you, sir. Most of them don't the first night out."

McBride decided he would, anyway. He had a new dinner coat he wanted to try out. Back in his own room he rang for Simmons. He was running the water in his tub when the steward came in. "Yes, sir?"

McBride studied the brick-red face with frank skepticism. "How are you fixed for brains, Simmons? Got any?"

Simmons made a mouth eloquent of self-disapproval. "Would I be a steward if I had?"

McBride nodded affably. "That's always a good sign, pal. A guy that admits he's dumb is usually pretty smart." He sat down on the divan and began unlacing his brogues. "How would you go about finding a couple of guys who might be aboard under names not their own?"

Simmons looked a little startled. "Friends of yours, sir?"

"In a way," McBride said. He yawned. "Yep, in a way you might call them that." He removed a sock, looked at it with frank distaste. Simmons went into the bath and turned the water off. When he came back McBride was standing beside the dresser. He had the pictures of Fenner and Teal in his hands. "You might take these along, Simmons. In your spare time look around. See some of your pals. I've an idea these gentlemen, if they're with us at all, will be traveling cabin class, not first. It would look a little funny for me to be making inquiries, don't you think?"

"Oh, yes, sir," Simmons agreed. "Very queer indeed, sir." He licked his lips. "I hope you don't mean these gentlemen any harm, sir?"

McBride laid a kindly hand on Simmons' shoulder. "My word on it, pal. I just want to know if they're aboard and where they're staying. Can do?"

Simmons had quite a struggle of it. You could see him remembering McBride's two guns. Finally, though, he made up his mind. He looked McBride straight in the eye. "You may depend on me, sir." He accepted the two prints with hands that trembled just a trifle.

McBride beamed. "Good boy, Simmons. I shall always remember you as the man who had but one life to give for his country." He winked. "And no unnecessary talking, Simmons. I don't want anybody but you to know I'm interested."

Simmons was overwhelmed. "Depend on me, sir," he said again. He went out. McBride repaired to the bath, feeling that he had earned a good day's pay. He made great splashing sounds as he tubbed, and roared a ribald song about a lady in Brazil who died possessed of great wealth because she valued her virtue highly. He was hardly thinking of Sheila Mason at all any more. He decided he might even get very drunk after dinner, so that he would be sure not to think of her, and to sort of prepare himself against a hard day tomorrow. The sweet clear notes of the dinner bugle swelled and died in the corridor as he dried himself.

AND SUDDEN DEATH, VI

THE main dining saloon was already crowded when McBride got down. It was a tall room, two decks high in the center, paneled in white and pastel shades below, a continuous series of shallow arches above. In the arches were murals, apparently done by someone who knew his stuff. McBride was not exactly a connoisseur of the fine arts, but he had never seen anything better in the Los Angeles Biltmore. A string orchestra was partially hidden behind great banks of ferns and fresh-cut flowers, and before the stage was a pool fed by twin fountains almost as magnificent as the one in McBride's Hollywood court. The fountains made him feel perfectly at home.

He found he had drawn a seat at F-9, a table for six rather far down the great room but in the middle section. A rosy-cheeked kid who turned out to be the fourth officer performed the introductions. There was an elderly couple named Carmichael and a woman named Smythe, who looked as though she might be a buyer for one of the better department stores, only she was going in the wrong direction for Paris.

McBride bowed politely. He wondered who belonged in the empty chair at his right. Mrs. Carmichael was on his left. It was odd how things kept cropping up to remind him of Sheila Mason and the Palos Verde dam case. There had been a couple named

Carmichael in that too, though the resemblance ended with the name. He attacked his shrimp cocktail with relish.

After a little while the talk became general, and, as seemed inevitable these days, finally got around to the prospect of war. "Those Japs," Mr. Carmichael said gloomily, "they're just biding their time." He looked at McBride. "Native of California?"

McBride said he was. He was not particularly proud of it, because they have a rather obscene song about what constitutes a Native Son and a Native Daughter.

"Well," Mr. Carmichael said accusingly, "what are you going to do about California's tremendous Japanese population?"

McBride said that he, personally, wasn't going to do anything about it. He said, "Most of them are better citizens than I am. They've found a hell of a good place to live, and if you think they're going to let anybody, even their Tokyo cousins, take it away from them you're crazy."

Mr. Carmichael looked at his wife to see whether she approved or disapproved of McBride's "hell." He couldn't quite make up his mind, so he followed her example and ate his fish. The Smythe woman winked at McBride. He thought maybe she was going to be all right. The pink-cheeked young officer, very handsome and scrubbed-looking, stood up suddenly. "Our sixth," he said happily. McBride saw a steward escorting Mrs. Nordstrom down the room. He didn't know how the fourth officer could have known she was Mrs.

Nordstrom. Apparently there had been an interchange of signals that he had missed. He stood up, as did Mr. Carmichael.

She was even more stunning than her pictures. Perhaps it was her gown, a black-and-silver effect that could have been painted on her. Her hair was platinum, her eyes a curious shade that might have been described as sea green. Her hips moved with a provocative sway that was just short of being a challenge. If McBride hadn't known he would have judged her as something under thirty. The four or five additional years had been kind to her. His eyes glowed warmly. "How do you do, Mrs. Nordstrom?"

She inclined her head. "Mr. McBride." She acknowledged the rest of the introductions with casual politeness. They sat down. The fourth officer was palpitant; Mrs. Carmichael suspicious and watchful of her husband, who flushed embarrassedly every time he caught her eye; Miss Smythe was faintly amused. McBride, terrifically conscious of Sybil Nordstrom on his right, was nonetheless able to pretend a stolid interest in his filet. Her perfume was faintly reminiscent of jasmine after nightfall.

The fourth officer—his name was Rhys—became very entertaining indeed. He pointed out various minor celebrities aboard, commented on the music, the weather, practically everything under the sun. Mrs. Carmichael ate determinedly, her evident intent being to get full value out of her passage money. Her husband sulked. Miss Smythe looked like the kind of woman who would enjoy one of McBride's barbershop anecdotes but he refrained from trying it out. Anyway, she was across the table and he was a little afraid of Mrs. Carmichael, on his left.

Mrs. Nordstrom said, "Who is that stunning woman in green at the captain's table?"

McBride craned his neck. The stunning woman in green at the captain's table was Miss Ford. She was not only at the table, she was directly beside the great man himself. She hadn't been there when McBride came in. She must have come down afterward. He opened his mouth to say something, but the eager-to-please Rhys beat him to it. "A Miss Ford, I believe. A Miss Kay Ford, of Los Angeles."

Mrs. Nordstrom raised her eyebrows. "Traveling alone?"

"I believe so."

She gave McBride a sidelong glance out of her sea-green eyes. "Competition, don't you think?"

"Not for you," McBride said gallantly. He almost said, "Not for you, babe." He'd been calling her picture "babe" for quite a while now. He looked at her right hand, trying to visualize a .32-caliber gun in it, the one that had snuffed out the life of the maid. The red nails winked at him, like the eyes of malicious little devils. He sighed.

Mrs. Nordstrom moved her excellent shoulders in an impatient shrug. "I must say you don't seem very interested."

"Oh, but I am!" McBride assured her.

"In Miss Kay Ford, of Los Angeles?"

"In you," McBride said. He meant this. He would have meant it even if he didn't think she was leading him toward two million dollars. Their eyes met briefly, then she was turning away to answer some remark of the ubiquitous Rhys. Little prickles of anticipation ran up and down McBride's spine. This job wasn't going to be such a chore, after all.

In the conversation which brought the meal to an end McBride discovered that Mr. Carmichael was in the sand and gravel business. Miss Smythe, whom McBride had thought might be a department store buyer, was, it developed, a writer for something she called the love pulps. She said she wrote under the name of Beulah Poindexter. McBride told them, with an eye to furthering his acquaintance with Sybil Nordstrom, that his father had left him a couple million and he wasn't doing anything at all for a while. Mrs. Carmichael thawed perceptibly. Sybil Nordstrom offered no information whatsoever about herself.

Excusing himself presently, McBride stood up and made his way forward, past the captain's table. There were eight diners here, seven besides the skipper. Miss Ford seemed to be doing all right for herself. She had the captain in stitches, and on her other side was a tall, very blond, very British young man who affected a monocle and an absorbed interest in everything Miss Ford did or said. The Baron Ito Itsuki waved a hand and McBride waved back. He ignored Miss Kay Ford of Los Angeles. There was, he told himself, not a jealous bone in his body, and besides, if she wanted to chase after every available male aboard ship, that was her business. He was scowling blackly as he rode the elevator up to B deck.

Simmons was hovering in the port passage. He had the air of a conspirator. "May I speak with you a moment, Mr. McBride?"

McBride unlocked his door. "Come in, pal, come in."

Simmons peered up and down the corridor before darting in and closing the door behind him. He removed the two pictures from beneath his starched coat. "I've found them, sir. At least I've found one of them." He stabbed a finger at Mr. George Teal's likeness. "This one."

"So?" McBride said. "Just like that, hunh?"

Simmons gulped. "He was in the cabin-class dining room. I thought the dinner hour would be a good time to look, so—"

"Excellent, Simmons," McBride said. "Then you had to ask no one else about them, eh? That's good. That's very good indeed, pal. I shall reward you." He took a twenty-dollar bill from his case.

Simmons was again overwhelmed. "That isn't necessary, sir. I—I rather enjoyed it, you know." His eyes admired the cut of McBride's dinner jacket. "If I may say so, sir, it's rather like being a detective, isn't it?"

McBride tossed the prints in a drawer. "I wouldn't know, pal. Detecting is a little out of my line."

Simmons winked. He was, you could see, not to be

fooled by McBride's offhand manner. "Oh, of course, sir. I understand. Quite." He giggled. "You're Mr. Capone, with his face lifted." He now became very confidential indeed. "The party I saw is in 411, port side, Deck D. I followed him up from the saloon."

McBride pressed the twenty on him. "Thanks, pal."

"And shall I continue my investigations, sir?"

McBride shook his head. "I wouldn't, pal. You'll lose your job, running around where you've no business to be."

Simmons was disappointed. "But it's no trouble, sir!"

"Forget it!" McBride said sharply. Immediately sorry, he put a hand on Simmons' shoulder. "You've done swell, keed. Don't overdo it." He pushed the little man out the door. It was only after he had been alone in the cabin for a few moments that he became aware of something wrong. Careless in many things, he was meticulous about his clothes and personal effects. It was a sort of fetish with him, when changing, to put discarded objects away as though he might have to find them again in total darkness. Whoever had searched his cabin had been careful, but not quite careful enough.

He stood there a moment, one hand on a tweed topcoat, eyes on the brown brogues he had taken off just before dinner. There were seven pairs of shoes on the floor of the wardrobe. The brogues should have been at the end of the row. Instead of that they were in the middle. There were other little signs too, now that he really began to look for them. Cursing fluidly, with the ease of long practice, he went about the business of checking for possible losses. There were none.

Quite suddenly he began to shake. Instead of easing him, the fact that there was nothing missing made him angrier than ever. It had been the same in the search of his court apartment back in Hollywood. Nothing gone, just somebody taking a hell of an interest in Rex McBride. Who it could be, or what it was that was being sought, was beyond him. As from a clear sky it came to him that the vandal might be Kay Ford. Come to think of it, she had admitted stopping by his place in Hollywood. Raging, he flung open his door and started out. Kay Ford was just passing. With her was the tall blond Britisher and his monocle. "Kay!" McBride said harshly.

She paused. "Yes?"

"I want to talk to you."

"All right, Rex, in a few moments." Her nod linked the two men. "Mr. Fessenden, Mr. McBride."

McBride ignored the Britisher's hand. He looked at Kay. "Not in a few moments. Now."

Fessenden excused himself hastily. Kay followed McBride over the threshold, watched him bang the door. Then, very deliberately, she struck him across the mouth. Her blue eyes were blazing. "You can't talk to me that way, McBride. Not even when we're alone. I won't have it."

He couldn't believe it for an instant. The sting of her knuckles was sharply insistent and the salt taste of blood was on his teeth and he still couldn't believe it.

"You tramp!" he said thickly. "You two-timing tramp!"

She would have struck him again, only this time he was watching. He caught her wrists in his two hands and held her there, at arm's length, until she ceased to struggle. Presently he began to laugh. "Why, you gorgeous hellcat!"

She was still angry. "I meant what I said, Rex. I won't have people think that I'm—that you're——"

Instantly he was contrite. "Damn it, kitten, I didn't think. I was so mad I couldn't think. Tell Fessenden I don't know any better. Tell him I'm a heel. Tell him I'm your country cousin, or anything you like, but for Christ's sake don't look at me like that!" He took a breath. "Would it help any if I apologized to the guy?"

In many ways Kay Ford was as volatile as McBride himself. Freeing her wrists she moved across to the dresser. In the mirror he saw that her eyes were laughing at him. "What's so funny?"

"You are," she said. She tossed him a clean handkerchief, watched him dab at his mouth. "You can dish it out but you can't take it."

He stared at her. "Meaning Fessenden?"

"Meaning Fessenden."

He began to laugh. "So you thought I was sore because you were with him! Well, blow me down."

"Well, weren't you?"

"Hell, no." He suddenly remembered what it was that he had been sore about. "Listen, what's the idea of snooping in my stuff? First Hollywood, now here. A fine thing!"

It was her turn to stare. "I don't know what you're talking about."

"Don't give me that!" he snarled. "You admitted you were at my place last night. Only I was too dumb to think of it at the time. So what the hell do you think you're looking for?"

She made a little gesture of disdain. "Don't be an ass, Rex. It's bad enough to be a boor, but I've always given you credit for at least a modicum of common sense."

He flushed under her calm gaze. "All right, then, who did it? Somebody practically wrecked the apartment. Here they were a little more subtle, but just as——" He broke off to stride across the room and lift the top mattress on the bed. The prints, the four he had not given to Simmons, were undisturbed. He sighed, not with relief particularly, because the mystery was still unsolved.

Miss Ford was watching him. "See here, Rex, I don't know what you are working on. You needn't tell me unless you wish. But something has occurred to me that might have a bearing."

"Well?"

She hesitated. "Well, last night when I stopped by your place there was a man loitering between your unit and the next. He didn't hear me coming and I saw him quite plainly. He was a Japanese. Does that make sense?"

"I'm damned if it does," McBride said. He frowned. "Not that I haven't been hearing enough about how the Japs are going to take us over one of these days." And then, for no reason at all except that Kay had mentioned a Japanese loiterer in the immediate vicinity of his apartment, he had a brief mental flash-back to sailing time that afternoon and his meeting with Baron Ito Itsuki. There had been at least a dozen people with binoculars at the rail. Why had Itsuki singled out McBride?

"Look," he said, "you had dinner with a Jap tonight. Was he the guy you saw?"

Miss Ford was startled. "Baron Itsuki? My goodness, no. This man was short and squat and ugly as sin. I thought he might have been the gardener."

McBride nodded. "Okay, babe, we'll have to write off the Yellow Peril, I guess. We would have, anyway." He grinned. "I'm working on the Nordic race, myself."

"I noticed," Miss Ford said caustically. "Beautiful, isn't she?"

McBride scowled. "If that's a crack you can tell Fessenden I don't think so much of him, either."

AND SUDDEN DEATH, VII

THE ship was motionless. It was probably this absolute cessation of forward movement which awakened McBride. He lay there for a little while in the darkness, orientating himself, listening for some sign that would tell him why they were lying to. On the promenade outside his windows there was movement, not hurried, but somehow purposeful. In the passage beyond his door there was the sound of voices, muted, as though the speakers were afraid of wakening near-by sleepers. In neither of these things could McBride detect a vestige of the panic which is usually associated with catastrophe at sea. He switched on his reading lamp and looked at his watch. It was two in the morning. He had been asleep for almost three hours.

He sat up and lit a cigarette, finally put on slippers and a robe and went to the door. Someone knocked lightly. He opened up and found himself looking at young Rhys, the fourth officer. Rhys was definitely older now, and some of the color was missing from his cheeks. "Pardon me," he said stiffly, "I just wanted to be sure you were all right." He turned away.

McBride caught his arm. "Wait a minute. Why shouldn't I be all right?"

Rhys looked at him. "Just a routine check-up, sir." He went on down the passage. Looking out, McBride saw that there were others, like himself, apparently awakened and donning the first thing that came to hand. Kay Ford, in satin mules and a negligee of some filmy white material, stood just outside her own door. In this particular section of B deck the cabins were all outside, built around a well which was solidly paneled and unbroken save for three doors marked: "Trunk Storage." Twin passages opened on a foyer at either end, but the center well made it impossible to see what was going on at the far side of the ship. There was a uniformed man stationed at each foyer entrance. Three or four passengers beside McBride and Miss Ford stood in their stateroom doors, but everyone seemed intent on utter quiet. Rhys had disappeared.

"What goes on?" McBride demanded. His voice sounded boomingly loud in the corridor. Everyone looked at him as though he had violated a grave.

Kay Ford came and stood beside him. "We don't know," she said. She shivered a little. "We've been like this for almost half an hour. I think I heard boats being lowered."

McBride went back into his room and got cigarettes. He lit one for her and they stood there beside his door, smoking quietly. "Nothing out on the promenade," he said presently. "I looked."

She nodded. "Must be on the other side." She shivered again, and McBride, frankly uncaring of what the others might think, put an arm around her. She leaned against him. "Why can't we be like this always, Rex?"

The perfume of her hair was like wine in his nostrils. "I don't know," he said gloomily. Perhaps it was the hour, or the unaccustomed surroundings which moved him to an admission he might not have made otherwise. "I've been thinking about what you said, kitten. Back there at the Grove. I fully intended to get drunk last night, but I didn't. I thought about you and me instead."

"And—her?"

He knew she meant Sheila Mason, and was suddenly embarrassed before her. This woman beside him had taken him and helped him over the first hump; with her eyes wide open, knowing him to be in love with someone else, she had deliberately given of herself to ease that first shock of bitter disillusion. What little self-respect he had left was due to her and he knew this now and was ashamed.

"A little," he confessed. "A guy like me can't toss it all overboard in a minute. Maybe you're right, though. Maybe I was just sore because she fooled me."

"I know," she said. She gave him a faintly tremulous little smile. "I'm sorry I hit you last night, Rex."

He grinned down at her. "I had it coming, hon. Being born in the gutter is something else you don't get over right away." He dropped his arm as Rhys came back along the passage. "So what did you find out? Are we sinking or just afire?"

"Neither," Rhys said. His eyes looked harried. "We're proceeding immediately."

"Well, for Christ's sake," McBride said, "is it a secret or something? Doesn't a first-class passage entitle me to know why the train stalled?"

Rhys shrugged tiredly. "We've lost a man overboard if you must know. We haven't been able to find him."

Miss Ford uttered a little cry. McBride cursed. "Who was it?"

"A steward," Rhys said. "A man named Simmons."

McBride sucked in his breath. Catching sight of his face in the polished panel across the passage he saw that it was almost dead white. He wet his lips. "You're sure?"

"Quite sure," Rhys said. "The deck-watch heard something, Simmons' cry, perhaps. All that was actually seen was an arm disappearing in the wake. Simmons didn't answer his emergency call to station."

McBride was still grasping at straws. "But he might have been sick or something. Hell's fire, man, Simmons was my own steward. I—I knew him!"

Rhys shook his head. "We've checked. Everyone else is accounted for."

McBride ran into his cabin and yanked open the drawer in which he had tossed the pictures returned to him by Simmons. They were not there. He knew then; knew that Simmons had gone on being an amateur detective. He was suddenly and violently sick.

After a time he came out of the bath. The nausea was gone, but Simmons' face wasn't. It seemed to be there before McBride's eyes, no matter where he turned, an eager, freckled face, rather apologetic and a little admiring. Hoping to blot the sight of it out by a mere physical act McBride stretched out on the bed and buried his face in a pillow. It was a horrible thing, this feeling he had. No matter how you looked at it, Simmons' death could be laid at no other door than Rex McBride's. You could say it was the little guy's own fault; he hadn't been satisfied to let well enough alone. But what good was that? If McBride hadn't given him a job to do, if he had never taken Simmons on in the first place, this thing could not have happened.

Then too, there was the manner of his passing. McBride had seen men die, most of them violently. Some of these deaths he himself had been directly responsible for. But just to vanish, an upflung arm in a churning sea of foam, then—nothing. Or was there something? Was there a little man somewhere out in that vast waste, all alone, so very alone, fighting the drag of his clothes, perhaps crippled, praying for the help that would never come?

McBride was not a crying man, but something very like a sob shook him now. The *Honolulu Queen* was again under way. It isn't fair, he thought, leaving him out there like that. By God, it isn't fair! And in the same breath he knew that everything had been done that could possibly be done. Master and officers and men were trained for things like this. They wouldn't have quit until the last chance was gone.

Presently someone knocked on McBride's door. He didn't get up, didn't even answer. The door opened anyway. He turned then, furious, and saw that it was Kay Ford. The anger went out of him as suddenly as it had come. "Oh, it's you."

She had changed to a tweed skirt and sweater. "I heard you being sick. I thought I'd better wait a little while." She came over and laid cool fingers on his forehead. "Don't you think we'd better talk things over, Rex?"

He wouldn't look at her. "What things?"

From beneath sullen lids he could see her mouth quiver a little. Her blue eyes were dark with compassion. "What things?" he repeated.

She sat on the edge of the bed. "I know you, Rex. Sometimes I think I know you better than you know yourself. The little man, Simmons, you feel responsible for him, don't you?"

He was angry, because it was even as she said. She could read him like an open book. "Why should I?" he asked roughly.

"I don't know that, Rex. I don't know why it should be so; I only know that it is. In some way he was mixed up in this case you're working on, wasn't he?"

McBride got up and took a turn about the room. "All right, he was." He told her about Simmons and the locating of George Teal down on Deck D. "He should have stopped there. I told him to forget it." He looked down at the spread palm of his right hand. "But no, he had to go on. He came back and lifted the pictures out of the drawer there, probably hoping to find Fenner too. And he got caught at it."

Miss Ford watched him. "Then you must know who got him, Rex."

McBride's eyes were feverish. "These guys are smart. Maybe they weren't once, but a couple of years in stir will make anybody smart—or stir-crazy." He cursed. "Of course I know who got him! It was either Teal or Fenner, or both."

"Then you'll notify the proper authorities?"

He looked at her. "What do you think? I haven't got an ounce of proof to offer. There's no rap against these guys. They've already served their time." He snapped his fingers. "Suppose I go to the captain and tell him what I've got? Hell, I haven't got anything. I haven't even got the pictures any more. Without an eyewitness there's not a chance in the world of convicting these guys. There's not even a body. Who shall say that the little guy didn't just jump?"

Her mouth made a firm straight line. "You're not letting it go because an investigation at this time might jeopardize your other interests?"

McBride caught her roughly by the shoulders. "You really do think I'm a heel, don't you?" He thrust her from him. "I'm not letting it go. The maid, yes. I didn't know her. But this is kind of a personal matter, hon. I'm taking care of it—personally."

She touched his arm. "These—these men. Has it occurred to you that Simmons may have been made to talk—first? That possibly they will try to do something about you?"

He laughed savagely. "I hope they do, hon. It will give me the chance to blast their guts out and ask questions afterwards." He got a sweater, slacks and sneakers from the wardrobe and went into the bath. When he came out he shoved his smaller gun, a .32 automatic, in his right-hand pants pocket. "I think I'll take a little turn up on A deck. Come along?"

They went out and up one of the forward companions beside the elevator. Passing through the foyer which gave on the lanai suites McBride chanced to look down the port passage leading to Number 8. The Baron Ito Itsuki was just backing out of Sybil Nordstrom's door.

AND SUDDEN DEATH, VIII

DAY, for McBride, usually dawned around ten o'clock. He was surprised to note, on awakening this morning, that it was only a little after eight. A burnished brass sun, reflected from the white paint of the promenade rail outside his windows, sent prying little slivers of light through the curtains to pluck at eyelids heavy from too little sleep. He had tramped the deck till almost five, long after Kay Ford had finally given up and gone down to her own cabin.

He lay there for a little while, smoking the inevitable before-rising cigarette, considering the events of the night, which were many, and his deductions concerning them, which were few. Three hours' sleep hadn't seemed to clarify the situation to any appreciable extent. It had all seemed so simple at first. It was believed that Sybil Nordstrom was on her way to meet her absconder-husband, and to share with him his ill-got gains. McBride, engaged to follow her, was to—if possible—see to it that the two million dollars was diverted into the coffers of the Monolith Corporation. If, in the doing thereof, he could also manage to put the cuffs on Nels Nordstrom, well and good.

Mr. Vickers of the Monolith Corporation had said there might be a little competition. It was unfortunate that he hadn't know how much. McBride made a bitter mouth at the thought of how little Vickers had actually known. He crushed his cigarette out in the tray at his elbow, swung bare feet to the floor. He wished he had a drink.

Strong brown fingers massaged his scalp as he considered the rest of the problem. There was the shooting of the maid. The obvious conclusion was that Sybil Nordstrom had discovered she was being spied upon and, either with deliberate intent or in a moment of panic, had written the maid off. Having met Sybil Nordstrom, McBride didn't think so much of the panic theory. She didn't look like the type to go haywire over a little espionage. She'd had too much of it in the years following the crash; the legitimate kind. Still, with a woman, anything was possible. Waiting for years for some word of her husband; finally getting it; you couldn't blame her if she lost her head a little. Against this you had Vickers' word for it that she had played her undeniable charms against the money of various men about town. This didn't exactly jibe with the picture of a grieving pseudo-widow.

But if Sybil Nordstrom had not done for the maid, then who had? Fenner? Teal? The O'Connor girl? McBride snapped his fingers in sudden memory. Here was Chalice O'Connor on the same deck with him and he hadn't done a thing about her! Was it possible that she, subbing for her prisoned father, was in league with Fenner and Teal? Had they formed a sort of alliance for the purpose of vengeance, or gain, or both? Did she know that Teal was aboard, and probably Fenner too? Did they know that she was? Here, Mc-

Bride decided, was another interesting angle. As if the thing weren't complicated enough!

Well, so maybe one of these three had killed the maid. Almost certainly one of them had killed Simmons, the steward. It couldn't have been Sybil Nordstrom, because Simmons wasn't interested in her. Or was he? Had he perhaps caught sight of her picture among the others when McBride had first sent him looking for Teal and Fenner?

"Christ!" McBride groaned. "Back right where we started from!" Like a tiny thread running through the whole jumbled pattern was the intense and as yet unexplained interest in McBride himself: the search of his Hollywood apartment; the second, though more artful, search of his cabin aboard ship. Then too, there was this screwy Japanese angle. Now that he came to think of it, what would a Jap gardener be doing around the court so late at night? Not mowing the lawn, surely. And what the hell did Baron Ito Itsuki mean by backing out of Sybil Nordstrom's suite at two in the morning? McBride thought that probably he had been drinking too much lately; he was seeing Japanese wherever he turned, like pink elephants. Nevertheless he filed the two apparently unrelated incidents away at the back of his mind until such time—if any—as they began to fit in with the rest of it.

Shaving, he regarded his reflection in the mirror. He thought he looked a little like George Raft this morning. He admired George Raft. He admired Ed Robinson too, though he was glad he did not look like Ed

Robinson. He selected a gray-green gabardine suit and black-and-white sport shoes from the adequate assortment in the wardrobe. No matter what developed in the way of mystery and sudden death you had to look your best. It was a matter of morale. McBride had not yet reached the point where he would admit right out that he was jittery, but his stomach had a funny way of jumping at unexpected sounds.

Before leaving the cabin he removed the four remaining pictures from beneath his mattress and studied them with varying emotions. Mr. George Teal evoked a straightening of the lips that boded little good for Mr. Teal. No longer in possession of a likeness of Saul Fenner, McBride dismissed Fenner with a shrug. He had met a few dangerous fat men in his time, not many. Frank O'Connor, being safely behind bars, was unimportant, save that his daughter was aboard and might possibly resemble the father. He spent a little more time on Nels Nordstrom, fixing the contours of the face and head in his mind, because it was quite possible that Nordstrom had altered his appearance since the taking of this picture. Sybil Nordstrom was the recipient of a blown kiss and the promise of something more satisfying to come. McBride now touched a match to the four prints and, holding them by an extreme corner until they were consumed, dropped the ash in the toilet and flushed it. He had the uncomfortable feeling that he should have done this before; it was a little like locking the proverbial barn door. But what privacy remained to him; what small chance there was of preserving at least a degree of secrecy regarding his mission, he desired to maintain as long as possible.

Feeling somewhat like the single goldfish in the bowl in the parlor he left his cabin and went down the passage to the foyer. Here he remained for a time, watching the parallel corridor, hoping to see Miss Chalice O'Connor come out of her stateroom. He was quite sure that he would know her, because he had previously ascertained the number of her cabin. She did not come out. No one did. Sighing, McBride rang for the elevator and descended to E deck and breakfast.

There was a paucity of customers in the main dining saloon this morning. McBride didn't know whether he was too late or too early. He thought that possibly there were a lot of breakfasters-in-bed, though how anybody could eat comfortably in bed had always been a mystery to him. More and more he was impressed with the fact that an ocean liner is little different from a hotel. The weather seemed to be holding excellent, and except for the slow, measured rise and fall of the floor under his feet McBride might have been in any one of a dozen Los Angeles restaurants. There was the same quietly efficient service, the same crisp napery, even fresh-cut flowers on the tables. The thirty or forty guests were well scattered, making the great room seem almost empty. At his own table McBride found no one but Sybil Nordstrom. Dishes not yet cleared away at two of the other places suggested that the Carmichaels had already eaten and gone.

Rhys, the fourth officer, must have been either asleep or on watch, nor was Miss Smythe in evidence.

Mrs. Nordstrom dawdled over her grapefruit. She was in a wool skirt and blouse and short Eton jacket, and her platinum hair was coiled close at the nape of her neck. She looked cool and competent and, McBride thought, beautiful as hell. Her sea-green eyes regarded him with interested amusement. "I tried to get you on the phone last night."

He pulled out his chair. "Did you?"

She nodded. "I was having a little party in my suite."

She's trying to tell me something, he thought. Without putting it into actual words. She didn't call me; probably she didn't have a party, either, but she wants me to think she did. Why? Then he got it. Not only had he seen Baron Ito Isuki, he had been seen. This was her way of accounting for the baron's presence. McBride tried to look as noncommittal as George Raft. "Oh?"

The steward appeared with her toast. McBride noticed that she ate it dry, without butter. "Yes," she said. "Itsuki is amusing, don't you think?"

McBride didn't bat an eyelash. "I've only spoken to him once or twice. Seems like a swell little guy." He gave his order to the steward. Then, turning, he met her eyes directly. "He say anything about liking to shoot craps?"

She said no, the baron hadn't mentioned craps. "Perhaps I could arrange something, though. Another night?"

"Any night," McBride said. His dark eyes admired her. "And you don't have to bother about the dice, either. I imagine you and I could find a lot to talk about."

Her slow smile was provocative. "Meaning we speak the same language, darling?"

He looked at her warmly red mouth. "I wouldn't be surprised." He attacked his kidneys and bacon with sudden vigor. "Nope, I wouldn't be at all surprised, Beautiful." His strong jaws moved rhythmically.

"I like the way you eat," she said after a while. "Is it true that you've got a couple of million dollars?"

He grinned at her. "Baby, I haven't got a dime. That was just for old sour-puss, the sand-and-gravel magnate's wife." He drank thirstily of his coffee. "Not a dime."

Mrs. Nordstrom moved her exquisite shoulders. "I still like you, darling." She rose. "Till later then?"

He did not get up. "Not too much later, Beautiful." He watched her move down the long room. The sway of her flat hips was a definite challenge now. He licked his lips.

As he was finishing his second cup of coffee a page came in from the main foyer. "Mr. McBride. Mr. Rex McBride!"

McBride lifted a hand. The boy had a radiogram. McBride tipped him, slit the envelope with a forefinger. The message was from Vickers: "Still no motive this end. Fingers right hand broken. Developments?"

McBride counted the words. Exactly ten. He cursed Vickers a little. So the autopsy had shown the maid's fingers to be broken. McBride laughed harshly. What Vickers had really meant was that no motive had been discovered by the police. The motive was there, all right. Both for the broken fingers and the subsequent shooting. The maid had been induced to talk before she was killed, but McBride still couldn't see how she had been able to do any talking about him. She hadn't known about him. Still, considering, he saw that it was possible the killer had traced him through Vickers. He got up and went out across the foyer to the telephone and radio central, where he filed a reply. "Good. Good. No."

As he paid for the gram the clerk handed him another. This one was from McGonigle and was a little more lavish than the one from Vickers. "Why wasn't I notified about accident aboard? Does it concern us? What the hell am I hiring you for?"

McBride, feeling the clerk's eyes on him, grinned embarrassedly. "These city editors!" He pulled a pad of forms toward him and indited another message: "McGonigle, *Tribune*, Los Angeles: Apparently you were. No. Are you?" Counting the words he saw that he had done even better than Vickers. This would never do. He tore off another blank and wrote recklessly: "McGonigle, *Tribune*, Los Angeles: Check on a Baron Ito Itsuki, supposedly attached to Japanese

Consulate, your city. He is taking me at pinochle." He passed the messages across the desk. "File those separately. I guess that'll teach him a lesson."

The clerk read the scrawls carefully. "You wish to pay for these?"

"Hell, no," McBride grinned. "Send 'em collect."

The clerk leaned across the counter. "I wouldn't tell you this, only I don't like Japs. Baron Itsuki has been making inquiries about you too."

"The hell he has!" McBride was delighted. "You're a nice guy, pal. Happen to remember who he asked?"

"The Japanese Consulate," the clerk said. He sighed. "I guess he really is a baron."

AND SUDDEN DEATH, IX

CENTERING the main foyer, directly opposite the elevator, was the purser's inquiry office. McBride stopped there and engaged one of the clerks in desultory conversation. "Traffic heavy this trip?"

It appeared that the *Honolulu Queen* was not by any means carrying a capacity load. The clerk was at a loss to understand it, he said. A nice boat, the right time of year, plenty of money in circulation. "Just an off trip, I guess." His eyes appraised McBride's clothes. "You're in 47, B deck, aren't you, Mr. McBride?"

"That's right," McBride said. He gave a very fair imitation of a man embarrassed no end. "Fact is, that's sort of what I wanted to inquire about." He coughed. "Would it be possible for me to engage another cabin?"

The clerk's eyebrows lifted a trifle. "Something wrong with the one you have, sir?"

"Oh, no," McBride said. "No, indeed." He became even more embarrassed. "That is, not exactly. You see—well, as a matter of fact, I write." He peered across the counter to see if the clerk was properly sympathetic. "We writers, you know, have our little peculiarities. Some people call them conditioned reflexes."

The clerk's manner became a mixture of official hauteur and overweening curiosity. "Yes, Mr. Mc-

Bride? Am I to understand that you wish to cancel your present reservation and make some other arrangement?"

McBride was horrified at the thought. "Oh no, indeed! I wouldn't think of it. But suppose I were to engage an additional passage. Would that entitle me to another cabin? Something not too expensive?"

"You mean you will want *both* cabins?"

"That's the general idea," McBride confessed. "Silly, isn't it?" He watched the young man's hands tremble, getting out deck plans. They finally compromised—or at least the clerk thought it was a compromise—on Cabin Class 419, Deck D. Seeing that Mr. George Teal was in 411, McBride couldn't have done much better. He emerged from the deal the proud possessor of keys to not only his original cabin, but to a second. He was not only a first-class passenger, he was a cabin-class passenger. He half wished he had taken up engineering in his youth. He might then have been eligible for the stokehold too. He felt that he was making rapid strides in his plan for the annihilation of one George Teal. He hadn't forgotten the little steward, Simmons.

Funny thing about Simmons, he thought. No one had even mentioned the incident this morning. He wondered if losing stewards overboard was a common occurrence. Seeing a sign next the telephone central which said: "Chief Steward," McBride went over there. He introduced himself. "I feel pretty bad about Simmons, you know. What's being done about him?"

The chief steward was a ruddy-faced man with a

bulbous nose in which a tiny network of broken veins reflected a misspent youth. "What can be done? He's just gone." He snapped his fingers. "Like that."

"They find the spot where he went over?"

"No." The chief avoided McBride's stare. "It is thought likely that he went off the cabin-class promenade on C-deck; possibly from the port side of B."

McBride was irritated. "Damn it, all the promenades I've seen around this boat have got rails at least four feet high. A guy doesn't just trip over a four-foot fence!"

The chief bridled. "See here, sir, I've already taken a beating from my superiors. I may get set down for it." The veins in his nose throbbed resentfully. "That's what you get for being kind-hearted!"

McBride scowled. "I don't get it."

The chief got out of his chair. "Simmons was a heavy drinker, mister. I knew that when I signed him on, but I took a chance because I was sorry for him. The investigation brought out this—this affliction of his, and consequently I have come in for a large share of the blame."

"But Christ, the rail is still four feet high!"

The chief looked at him. "Whisky does funny things to a man, mister." He became sadly reminiscent. "Once, when I was an apprentice——"

"Save it!" McBride snarled. He swung on a heel and crossed the foyer to the stairs. It was beginning to look as though all his thoughts of vengeance, all his plans, were wasted. Simmons, if you could believe the chief steward, was a lush, and probably, while in his cups, reverted to type and imagined himself one of Darwin's monkeys. Only his tail hadn't been long enough.

McBride felt himself cheated. There were still the missing pictures, of course, but you couldn't be sure Simmons hadn't taken them along on the fatal dive. McBride's private opinion was still unchanged, but he was a fair man. He would have to have more than just the absence of the photographs before he knocked off even a guy like Teal. The entire ship's complement was apparently satisfied to make a report to the owners and let it go at that. Incidentally, that must have been how McGonigle got the news—through the owners. McBride cursed McGonigle wholeheartedly. Even four or five hundred miles away, the guy seemed to know as much about what was happening as did McBride himself.

At the head of the stairs McBride turned right and went aft by way of the starboard passage. He had to go through three sets of doors to get to the one marked Cabin Class. He was in a mood to be a trifle communistic and his lip lifted at the assumption that the mere possession of an additional hundred dollars marked the difference between a sheep and a goat. Cabin Class passengers, he gathered.

Coming into the cabin-class foyer he found it but a smaller, less ornate replica of the first class. Here were the cabin purser's office, the cabin steward's office and the ship's doctor. Transverse passages, leading from the main ones, gave on the staterooms. 419 was an inside cabin, cornering the main starboard and the first lateral. From its door McBride could see part of the foyer, including the purser's office, and certainly he had an excellent view of 411, supposedly housing Mr. George Teal. It was directly opposite. He identified himself at the desk, where he was told that all arrangements had been made from above. The man who told him this obviously believed him a screwpot. McBride almost concurred with this opinion. Entering 419 he found two berths, no bath. There was, however a private toilet. He was relieved.

For one who had never been aboard anything bigger than the Catalina Island steamers McBride had a very comprehensive picture of this one in his mind. He was what is known in theatrical parlance as quick study. Besides, practically every motion-picture opus he had seen in the last six months had had at least one ocean voyage in it, and this, together with his surveys of deck plans, room plans, and one thing and another, made him almost letter-perfect.

For instance, he was convinced that for a cabin-class passenger to get into any of the first-class sections would be no easier than for the fabled rich man to get into the kingdom of Heaven. Whether or not this worked in reverse he didn't know. Hence the cabin-class reservation. He had wanted to be in a position to come and go as he pleased without having to answer questions. But now that he was here, and having learned that Simmons might have come to his untimely end through John Barleycorn instead of George Teal, he was a little at a loss to chart his next move.

From his initial observations it seemed inconceivable that Simmons could have been killed, or even attacked, in Teal's stateroom. The lateral passage ended in nothing bigger than a porthole, for here on D deck there was no outside promenade except for a small section aft. Obviously you couldn't thrust a man through a porthole. And to reach the after promenade you would have to first negotiate the open foyer and one of the main passages. Presumably there was someone on duty in the various offices, no matter what the time of night, but even if there weren't, a guy would be crazy to go dragging a body around in so public a place. McBride didn't think George Teal was crazy.

By means of a match he wedged his door open just a crack and sat on the edge of the right-hand berth. From this vantage point he could at least see anyone who entered or left Number 411. When, after half an hour, no one did, he became impatient and decided to expedite matters a little. He went to the phone and asked to be connected with Suite 62, on B deck. Then, draping a handkerchief over the transmitter, he waited for an answer. When it came he said in tones of extreme anguish, "You'd better get down here right away!" He depressed the hook instantly and returned to his seat by the door. He had to wait less than five minutes before a girl entered the passage and knocked on the door of 411. He had only a swift vision of her, and of the man who gave her admittance, but he was more than satisfied.

Not only had he located the enormously fat Saul Fenner in George Teal's cabin, he had proved beyond the shadow of a doubt that Chalice O'Connor was in league with them both.

AND SUDDEN DEATH, X

THE outdoor swimming pool on B deck, reached by way of the forward promenade and shallow tile stairs, was doing a nice business. The tile deck around the actual pool itself was liberally besprinkled with gay, umbrella-shaded tables and with guests no less gay and even more colorful. A couple of white-coated stewards were being kept very busy indeed serving tall cool drinks to those who, though clad for it, apparently thought swimming was just something to be watched. Half-a-dozen exuberant youngsters splashed water noisily.

McBride, at the rail, looked down upon this pleasant scene with a jaundiced eye, because at one of the tables Miss Kay Ford was being entertained by Fessenden, the tall blond Britisher with the monocle. Miss Ford was wearing trunks and a halter under an embroidered coolie coat, bright green clogs on her feet, and a green-and-white polka-dot bandanna was tied Aunt Chloe fashion about her blue-black hair. Little diamond-like drops of water still clung to her faintly golden legs. She had been in the water, then. Fessenden's bony shanks protruded from beneath a striped wool beach robe. His monocle winked in the sun. Overhead roared one of the giant clipper ships out of San Francisco. Her wings cast a fleeting shadow over the *Honolulu Queen*, everybody waved, then she was gone, a twinkling spark of silver on the horizon, no bigger than Fessenden's monocle. McBride removed himself to the starboard rail and stared with affected interest at the bow wave, far below, climbing away from the cut-water with indomitable though futile persistence. Accustomed to other forms of travel, it seemed incredible that they could have been going along like this for almost twenty-four hours and still be less than five hundred miles out of San Pedro. He wished that Sybil Nordstrom had chosen to fly instead. The Clipper would have been a little crowded, though, at that, he reflected, what with her normal complement plus Mrs. Nordstrom and himself, the inseparable Fenner and Teal and Miss Chalice O'Connor. For some reason he did not include the Baron Ito Itsuki in this purely imaginary flight. Perhaps this was because Itsuki seemed to have no definite place in the scheme of things. He was there, McBride thought sulkily, like some of the things a magician does with his left hand—just to make it harder.

All about him, strolling, reclining in deck chairs, were people interested in books, the weather, politics, and each other. McBride was suddenly and unaccountably lonely.

Miss Ford must have sensed this, for she paused on her way along the deck to touch his arm. "Good morning, Rex." Fessenden was still with her.

"Hello," McBride said. He looked at Fessenden's monocle. "You wear that thing in swimming too?" Miss Ford was terribly embarrassed for him. He grinned suddenly and stuck out a lean brown hand. "I'm a heel, fella. How's about forgetting last night and just now?"

Fessenden's bony freckled fist had a surprising amount of strength. "Quite," he said. Their hands dropped apart and they measured each other covertly. McBride decided that even a guy with a monocle could be a man. He accepted a loose cigarette from the pocket of Fessenden's floppy robe, and the three of them stood there talking for a few moments. They were still there when Baron Ito Itsuki passed by. Itsuki was wearing gray flannels. His small jet mustache made the inevitable V as he acknowledged McBride's wave. He had the whitest teeth McBride had ever seen.

Miss Ford said, "Handsome, isn't he?"

"I wish I had his tailor," McBride said.

Fessenden said nothing at all. His almost colorless eyes were fixed on a plume of smoke on the distant horizon. After a little while McBride excused himself. "Well, see you all later." He grinned at Fessenden. "And forget the cracks, will you? I'm not such a bad guy when you get to know me." He went along the promenade to the nearest door and from there to his cabin. His key would not turn in the lock.

Presently discovering that this was because the door was already unlocked he turned the knob quietly and went in. The latch of the bathroom door made the faintest possible click. Then there was no sound at all. He stood there for a long moment, nostrils flared a little, savoring the air. The sun, streaming through his windows, laid two broad bands of butter-yellow across the carpet. It was very quiet. McBride was not frightened. Rather, the affair promised to be amusing.

He deliberately chose a chair in a direct line with the bathroom door, sat in it, crossing his legs and lighting a cigarette. "All right," he said quietly, "you can come out now."

There was no answer. His voice became mildly persuasive. "I can wait just as long as you can, baby."

The door opened a bare six inches, and a hand and part of a wool-sleeved arm came through. The hand clutched a small pearl-handled gun. The hand was smaller than the butt plates; this was how McBride knew they were pearl. "Turn around," a smothered voice said. "Turn around and face the wall."

"Unh-unh," McBride said comfortably.

"I don't want to have to hurt you."

"I know you don't," McBride said. "That's why I haven't yelled for help. Besides," he added, "I know who you are, so you might as well come out and be sociable."

There was a quick indrawn breath, then the door was flung wide and Chalice O'Connor stood framed in the opening. Her face was flaming. She was a small girl, smaller than he had thought from the brief flash he had got of her outside George Teal's room. Copper-red hair caught the sun like the pot of gold at rainbow's end. Her eyes, unlike those of her father, were brown. McBride guessed her to be twenty, not over twenty-two. He was a little sorry for her.

He flicked ash from his cigarette. "You look like too nice a girl for this sort of thing, Chalice."

Again that quick indrawn breath. She was laboring under tremendous emotion. "So you do know who I am!"

"Of course. Now don't you think you'd better put that litle popgun in your pocket before it goes off and shoots somebody, maybe me, in the stomach?" He stretched long legs out in front of him. "You don't have to be afraid of me, kitten. I've been broke myself."

Sudden relief flooded her eyes. It was as though he had given her a reprieve, which, indeed, he had intended. If she happened to be that kind it was better for her to think him dumb than to know that he knew exactly why she was aboard. Her shoulders sagged a little. "All right, I'm a potential thief. What are you going to do with me?"

His eyes were warmly appreciative of her good looks. "Nothing."

She bit her lip. "Aren't you—aren't you even going to search me?"

"You said 'potential,' didn't you?"

She stared at him unbelievingly for a full minute. Then, with a tremulous little half-smile: "You're rather an amazing person, Mister—Mister Whatever-your-name-is." She stuffed the toy gun in her pocket. "By the way, how did you know me?"

"Your name on the passenger list," he said. "It has a musical sound to it. Later I had you pointed out to me, and still later I smelled your perfume. It was heavy in the air here when I came in."

Two bright spots of color burned high up in her cheeks at that. "You're still an amazing person."

"Of course," he said. "The name is McBride." He got up and went to the outside door. "May I ask how, of all the people aboard this lovely ship, you happened to choose me for your attention?"

"It was the key," she said. "I had an idea there might be more than one lock my own key would fit, so I just went around trying them."

"I see," he said gravely. He didn't believe her, but he pretended that he did. "I see." With his left hand he opened the door. His right he put under her chin, tilting her head up so that he could look deep into her eyes. "Remember what I said, Chalice O'Connor. You're too nice a girl." He bent to kiss her and it was then for the first time that he saw they had company. Miss Kay Ford was at her own door, regarding him with active dislike.

AND SUDDEN DEATH, XI

It was around five in the afternoon, teatime, and McBride, who cared very little about tea, had retired to his quarters on B deck, hoping to catch up on some of the shut-eye he had missed the night before. Fearing insomnia, because of the dozen-odd questions chasing themselves around in his mind, like mice, he had thoughtfully provided himself with a fifth of rye. He was not drunk, but he was in a mellow mood, viewing the world and all in it—with the possible exception of George Teal—as a kindly god does the poor unenlightened mortals who clutter up the earth. The fifth was only down about a quarter of the way.

Maybe Fenner is seasick, he thought drowsily. He was a little sorry for Fenner, having to live with George Teal like that. But just the same, both of them ought to be ashamed of themselves, making a nice kid like Chalice O'Connor do their dirty work for them. Obviously her appearance in his cabin indicated a certain knowledge on their part that he, McBride, was holding cards in the game. The only way they could have gotten this knowledge was through Simmons, who was now dead. If McBride had needed it, this was convincing proof that one or the other had killed him. He wondered if Chalice O'Connor was a party to the murder. He hoped not, because he was feeling very kindly toward Chalice. She had, he remembered, three freckles on her tip-tilted nose. Cute.

Sipping from the bottle, he was even disposed to feel magnanimous toward Miss Ford. Let her have her monocled Britisher Fessenden. She deserved him. He winced slightly, remembering the look on her face as he parted from Miss O'Connor. Then he became very angry indeed. It was all right for Kay Ford to make free of his cabin, but let anybody else do it and right away she got ideas. As if any girl, any old girl at all, wouldn't be as safe with him as—— He dozed off.

When he regained consciousness it was dark in the room and he thought at first that they were in the middle of a storm at sea. Then he saw the gleam of a starched white coat and knew it was only a steward shaking him. "Go away," he said crossly.

The steward went away as far as the nearest wall switch. Sudden light almost blinded McBride. "I thought so," the steward said. "I thought I reco'nized that name."

McBride peered nearsightedly. He saw a thick-set gorilla of indeterminate age, a man who if he wasn't a pug had every right to be. A cauliflower ear and a nose slightly askew gave him a somewhat waggish air. He wore his white coat without dignity. "Well," McBride said, "it's certainly been nice meeting you like this." He drank thirstily from the bottle. "Drop around again some time. Any time. But not now." He lay back on the pillows and closed his eyes.

"Meanin' you don't remember me?"

McBride rolled over so the lights wouldn't hurt his eyes. "Why should I? I never saw you in my life before."

"The hell you didn't!" this strange steward said. He pounded his barrel chest. "Me, The Diver, and he says he don't remember me." His voice lowered to cajolery. "Why, boss, you and me was on a party together once. At Packy O'Farrell's, 'member? I drank you under the table."

Obviously this was an out-and-out lie. Nobody could drink a McBride under the table, at least not and live to brag about it. He sat up and reached for the thermos jug. "You're a liar," he said pettishly. "You're just imposing on my known friendship for Packy O'Farrell." He poured some of the ice water in a cupped hand and applied it to the back of his neck. "Poor old Packy."

"Yeah," the steward said gloomily. He brightened. "Well, that's what he gets for tryin' to throw a fight two ways. It just ain't in the cards." He went into the bath and came out with a saturated towel which he wrapped around McBride's head. "Now, me, when the Commish says I'm through, I lam."

McBride was beginning to have a very hazy recollection of the affair in question. This guy had been one of O'Farrell's string, a boy whose only claim to fame was that he could make a dive convincing as hell. The commissioners had finally caught up with him. It was on the night of his last dive, after Packy's crowd had made a pot of money, that they fêted the kid. McBride had happened to be there.

"That was a long time ago," he said. "Must be all of five or six years." He removed the towel and began massaging his scalp, because it seemed quite numb. "Let's see, now, the name was Sweeney, right?"

The Diver nodded happily. "I knew you'd remember, pal. A dick like you is like a—now—elephant. He never forgets." He helped himself to a slug from McBride's bottle. "I always been a great admirer of yours, pal. Fact is, I was a dick myself for a couple of days. For the Cronin agency."

"That lousy outfit!" McBride sneered. He took his head out of his hands long enough to fix Sweeney with a bloodshot eye. "A hell of a steward you are!"

"You think I ain't?" Sweeney demanded indignantly. "Watch!" On the instant he became a servile creature, the epitome of all that is best in gentlemen's gentlemen. "Oh, quite, sir. Very good, sir." He waited for applause that didn't come.

"You've been seeing too many pictures," McBride said. He got up and went into the bath. When he came out he looked almost human. Sweeney was still there. The room reeked of rye whisky. "Before you get stinko," McBride suggested, "you might tell me how you got to be a steward, and how you got into this cabin, and why you were shaking me, and a few little odds and ends like that. I'll give you a break. I'll admit right off that you knew me when. Start from there."

Sweeney sighed. From his jacket pocket he took a

small tin of violet breathlets, helped himself to two and offered the tin to McBride, who shuddered violently. "No?" Sweeney shrugged. "Oh, well, I guess you don't have to, bein' a dick."

McBride glared at him. "I wish you could forget that for a while, pal. There aren't more than fifty or sixty people on this lousy tub that know about me. It's supposed to be a secret."

Sweeney winked prodigiously. "I catch, pal. You're on a big job and you're non compos mentis." He sighed enviously. "Jesus, what a life!"

"You said it," McBride agreed. He wondered what else could happen to him. He debated between white tie and tails and black tie and dinner coat. "As you were saying?"

"Well," Sweeney continued, "it's kind of a long story. On account of they wouldn't let me fight no place else I let myself get sucked into the Navy." He waved an expansive hand. "I seen the world through plenty portholes, pal, believe me. And I took plenty dives in the ring, too," he added aggrievedly, "and nobody gave a damn."

McBride was pulling on his pants. "That's swell, pal. So then the Admiral made you a steward."

"Well, no," Sweeney confessed. "That was after I quit the Navy. I got a job on a tanker that carried five-six passengers, and then I applied for a job with this line, only they were all full up on stewards, so I shipped as a seaman. And then last night this guy Simmons knocked himself off, so——"

McBride nodded. "That brings us right up to date, doesn't it? So now you can tell me how you got in and why you were trying to shake me loose from my teeth."

"All the room stewards has got master keys," Sweeney said. "That's on account of if there's a fire, or somebody knocks himself off, or like that." He smiled paternally on McBride. "So checking up on my twelve or fourteen rooms I run across your name, only I don't see you around all day, so I think maybe you got knocked off or something. You don't even show for dinner, so I come in and there you are." He drew his mouth down in patent disapproval. "Stinko!"

McBride denied this with some heat. "I was not. I was asleep."

"Yeah, asleep!"

McBride had decided on the white tie, because he had worn the dinner jacket last night and he wanted to impress Sybil Nordstrom. The master key was something he hadn't thought of; not as belonging to the steward, anyway. This was another link in the chain of evidence against Teal and Fenner, and possibly Chalice O'Connor too. The key she had used could have been taken from Simmons. He regarded Sweeney with a speculative eye. "Look, keed, you want to be a dick, hunh?"

Sweeney's eyes glowed. "You said it, pal!"

McBride shook his head. "No, I couldn't do it. You'd be like Simmons. You wouldn't be satisfied to just do as you're told. You'd have to go monkeying around till somebody handed you a bellyful of lead." He watched Sweeney's face covertly.

Sweeney licked his lips. "You mean some bastard got to Simmons? You mean it wasn't no accident?" He bunched his shoulder muscles till the starched coat crackled a warning. "Show me this guy, pal. Just point him out to me."

McBride shrugged. "You see? Right away you want to blow your top."

Sweeney relaxed. "I get it. Soft pedal, hunh? Undercover stuff." He reached for the bottle, thought better of it and took a violet instead. "Okay, pal, I can wait if you can. I 'member once, in the Navy, I laid for a guy for two whole cruises. There's never no hurry about a thing like that."

"No," McBride agreed. He wasn't horsing around now. His mouth was a straight hard line. "No, there's no hurry about a thing like that." He bent to wipe his patent-leathers with a towel. "I don't want you to do any thinking, fella. Thinking is what got Simmons. It's just that there's only one of me and I can't be in seven different places at once. So keep an eye on this cabin, will you? If you catch anybody—anybody—in here that don't belong, well——"

Sweeney made a chopping motion with his right hand. "I'll take care of it, pal."

"My guns are in the top drawer," McBride said. "I don't want you to take any chances. Just shoot and we'll fix up the story afterward."

Sweeney shivered a little. "You're a cold-blooded

fish. If you know who you're expecting, why don't you——?"

"Notify the captain?" McBride smiled. "No, Sweeney, I don't think we ought to bother the skipper. It will be so much nicer if our friend gets killed as, say, a prowler." He pointed an admonishing finger. "Always remember that, Sweeney. If you've got to kill a guy, try to do it lawfully." He shrugged his coat into a more perfect fit and went out to the elevator, descending presently to the main foyer. His friend at the radio desk waved frantically. McBride went over and accepted the blue-and-white envelope. The message was from McGonigle. It said: "Party well-known here. En route Yokohama. Coincidence his residence same address as S. N. Pinochle, hah-hah!"

McBride grinned engagingly at the clerk. "Good old McGonigle. He thinks I don't know how to play pinochle." As a matter of fact, he didn't know how to play pinochle, and McGonigle knew he didn't, and was thus able to read into McBride's message more than was actually said. Turning away, McBride remembered that he hadn't been the only one looking for information. He swung back to the desk. "What did our Japanese friend find out about me?"

"That you were a private detective."

"So?" McBride said. He peeled a twenty from the folded sheaf he carried in a pants pocket. The action, the denomination of the bill, reminded him that he had given one to little Simmons too. To take the curse off he put another with it, creased them inside a blank form and slid the form across the counter. "You happen to be watching his face when he read the message?"

"You can't tell anything about these Japs," the clerk said. "That's what scares me about 'em. Take this Itsuki, for instance. If I didn't know better I'd say he was tickled to death about you."

"Thank you," McBride said. He did not look tickled about the Baron Ito Itsuki.

AND SUDDEN DEATH, XII

It was quite late, almost nine o'clock, and though the foyer had been well filled the dining room was not. The orchestra still played and there were perhaps seventy or eighty scattered diners, but the big push was definitely over. McBride's delayed entrance, the ultramagnificence of his evening attire, was almost a total loss. At the captain's table Miss Ford still lingered, together with Fessenden, Baron Itsuki and a woman with white hair whom McBride hadn't noticed before. The captain himself was not present.

Passing down the left-hand aisle toward his own table McBride nodded distantly to Miss Ford and the others. Rhys, the fourth officer, was having coffee with Sybil Nordstrom. He stood up as McBride appeared. "Hello, there."

"Hello," McBride said.

"We were afraid you were ill."

"Oh, no, nothing like that." McBride sat and draped his napkin over a knee. He discovered that he was quite hungry. Presently Rhys made his excuses and went away. McBride attacked his shrimp cocktail.

Sybil Nordstrom sighed. "It seems the only time I can get a word with you is at the table."

"Busy," McBride said. He avoided her eyes.

"I'm having another little party tonight. After the dancing. May I count on you?"

McBride was busy with his fish. Apparently the steward was in a hurry to get away and the service was, if anything, too excellent. He paused to give her a warm stare. "I wouldn't miss it, Beautiful."

She rose, and perforce he did too. He hadn't done this at breakfast but he tried never to use the same act twice in a row. She was wearing plain black tonight, no jewels. Her platinum hair reminded him of the chromium tresses on the gal who adorned his car's radiator. He was not in an amorous mood tonight. He watched her halfway down the room before he resumed his dinner. The steak was without flavor.

After a little while he became conscious of a new presence at his elbow and looked up to see Fessenden standing there. His foot slid a chair out. "Sit down?"

"No," Fessenden said quietly. "No, I don't think I care to sit with you."

The tone, the words themselves, brought McBride to his feet instantly. "Why not?"

"Because, either consciously or unconsciously, you are a blackguard. You're not fit to wipe Kay Ford's shoes, yet you have the colossal cheek to actually flaunt your other women in her face, to entertain them in your——"

"You son of a bitch," McBride said. He was shaking. "You son of a bitch."

Fessenden hit him then. A handful of bony knuckles smacked McBride in the mouth, not hard, else McBride would have had to buy some new teeth. As it was he fell back against the table and dishes crashed to the floor. Straightening, with Fessenden's face a blurred target before his eyes, he forced himself to look down at his hands. They were clenched so tightly that the knuckles showed white. He watched them relax, the fingers leaving the marks of his nails in the flesh of the palms. It was as though they were another's hands, not his own. Presently he became conscious of voices around him and knew that the moment had passed in which he might have killed Fessenden. He was all right again. He laughed shortly. "Just a little accident, folks. My friend's foot slipped."

Beyond Fessenden, ringed by a dozen other faces, he could see Kay Ford's and Baron Itsuki's. Itsuki's was utterly devoid of expression. The back of Miss Ford's right hand was against her mouth and her blue eyes were wide and a little frightened. McBride touched a handkerchief to his lips. "Good night, all." He turned and went down the long room toward the main foyer.

Miss Ford found him after a time at the bar in the smoking room on A deck. She took the stool next him, ordering a Collins. "I'm sorry, Rex."

He didn't look at her. "Are you?"

"Fessenden is in love with me," she said. "People in love often do funny things; frequently things they are sorry for."

His eyes smoldered. "Is this an apology by proxy?"

She caught her breath. "You don't make it any easier for a girl, McBride."

"Should I?" He laughed harshly. "Shooting off your mouth to a guy like him!"

She pushed her Collins away, untasted. Music from the ballroom drifted into them, languorous, strong with the melody, the way McBride liked it. "You could give me hell, Kay, even stick a knife in me if you thought you had a beef coming. But to go blabbing to somebody else——"

"I know," she said. She picked up the Collins and drank thirstily. "I told you that people in love often do funny things. I was having a quiet little cry, all by myself, and Fessenden came around and—well, he *is* in love with me, and he had a nice broad shoulder." She looked at him. "How did I know he was going to turn into a charging knight?"

"I see," McBride said. He sipped straight rye.

She stood up. "I just wanted to tell you, Rex, that you were rather fine about the whole thing."

"I'll bet," he said gloomily. The music was making him sentimental as hell. He drew his brows down in a fierce scowl. "Damn it, hon, that girl this afternoon—she's part of what I'm working on. I caught her prowling my cabin."

Miss Ford's eyes were a little incredulous. "And you kissed her and let her go?"

He flushed angrily. "All right, then, the hell with you!"

She began to laugh then, a little hysterically, McBride thought. "You fool, don't you suppose I want to believe you? Do you think a woman like me can go on throwing herself at a man's head and not lose every vestige of pride?"

"I've got a certain amount of pride too," he said shortly. "The gutter kind. The kind that doesn't like to admit being wrong." He stood up. "Let's dance."

It was after the third or fourth number that the orchestra, by popular demand, began descending the scale to swing, and finally to boogie-woogie. McBride stopped stock still in the middle of the floor. "Let's get out of here. I don't know why they don't just give 'em all drums and let it go at that."

Miss Ford allowed herself to be dragged away. Out on the after promenade they leaned on the rail together, watching the moon silver the froth of the spreading wake. McBride, a little drunk from holding her in his arms, but not drunk enough for boogie-woogie, said irritably, "All right, smarty, for the sake of argument I'll admit you were right about Sheila Mason. She suckered me and I was sore. So what does that make you and me?"

She turned to face him, tilting her head back a little so that he could see her eyes. They were like pools, so darkly blue they seemed almost black. "You mean that, Rex?"

He kissed her, rather gently for him. After a while he released her and stared gloomily out over the climbing seas. "I wish I knew what in hell I've got that makes people want to do things for me." He told her about his new acquisition, Sweeney. "Here's a guy as crooked as a dog's hind leg. He's seen me maybe twice in his life, yet he's perfectly willing to take a chance in order to do me a favor. There was little Simmons, too. And you." He thought about this for a while. "It must be some kind of a curse."

"Or a blessing," Miss Ford said. "Has it ever occurred to you that people don't go on consistently liking a man who is as big a heel as you think you are?"

He grinned in spite of himself. "That's pretty complicated, hon. I'll have to reduce it to its essentials when I've got a little more time." His gloom returned. "A hell of a blessing that is, anyway! It's getting so that if I say more than a casual greeting to anybody they turn up with their throats cut. Or they don't turn up at all—like Simmons." He shivered. "It's a curse, I tell you!"

A strand of her hair blew across his face as she leaned toward him. "Not a curse, Rex. You mustn't think it."

"Then why do things always happen to me?"

"Like this?" She kissed him lightly. "Perhaps it's because you haven't quite grown up yet. You're still the little toughie who hustled papers around Los Angeles dives when other kids were in bed. You had to be tough to survive. You'll get over it."

He doubted this, but for the present he let himself be lulled into a sense of security, like when the doctor tells you it's only a belly ache, not appendicitis. He put an arm around her and they stood there for a while, close together, unashamed before the other couples who came and went around them. Briefly, he was quite happy.

It was Rhys, the fourth officer, who put an end to it. McBride turned at the touch on his arm. "Yes?"

"The captain would like to see you, Mr. McBride."

"What about?"

"I'd rather not say, sir." Rhys' manner was stiff, faintly hostile. His eyes looked harried. They ignored Kay Ford, slid away from McBride to encompass a second officer, just coming out of the ballroom. "We'd rather you went quietly, sir."

McBride looked at Kay. His eyes said, "You see?" Then, shrugging, he turned on Rhys and the other man. "Of course I'll go quietly. But I won't go at all," he added, "until you tell me the score." He chuckled derisively. "I've got to have time to think up the right answers."

Miss Ford said, "Rex!"

Rhys' face was white with anger. "All right," he said. "You've asked for it and I'll give it to you. You're wanted for the murder of Cecil, Lord Fessenden."

AND SUDDEN DEATH, XIII

ODDLY enough, Fessenden was in his own room. Oddly, because it seemed to McBride that nobody aboard the *Queen* stayed in his or her own quarters. There was Hepburn, the master, and his chief officer, whose name McBride did not know. There was Rhys, naturally, and the other man who had escorted McBride. The ship's doctor, identifiable because of the stethoscope dangling from his neck, was standing at the foot of the bed and making disagreeable sounds with his mouth. Last but not least there was Fessenden himself. He lay on the bed, face down, bony arms drooping on either side, naked to the waist. The condition of the little pile of clothes on the floor gave mute evidence that he hadn't undressed himself. There were two deep knife wounds in his back, about halfway down, slightly off center. McBride thought he must have died instantly, though he was later proved wrong about this. Fessenden had been still breathing when they found him.

Captain Hepburn cleared his throat. He was a ruddy-faced man, a little on the paunchy side, but quite handsome in his dress uniform. He had an iron-gray mustache which he worried with the index finger of his right hand. "Seems you had a quarrel with Fessenden this evening, Mr. McBride."

"He smacked me," McBride admitted.

"But you didn't hit him back?"

"No."

Hepburn gnawed at a fingernail. His eyes had the clarity of an ingenuous child's. "You saved your—er—reprisals till later?"

"Meaning that I killed him?"

"I think so," Hepburn said. He seemed a little put out about the whole thing. "We're waiting to hear your side of it."

He looked at the doctor. "When did it happen?"

"Perhaps an hour, possibly only a half. He was found on the port-side promenade about fifteen minutes ago. We have no means of knowing how long he'd been lying there, though the seaman who found him thinks he saw someone running from the spot."

"Seagram!" the captain said reprovingly. The doctor looked embarrassed.

McBride nodded. "It doesn't matter a great deal. I can account for all my time. From the dining room I went directly to the smoking-room bar, where I was joined by Miss Ford. After that we danced. We were still together when Rhys found us."

The captain looked at Rhys. "Check that, mister." Rhys went out. Nobody else did. It seemed that they were all afraid McBride was going to try to escape or something. The chief officer returned to his post by the door, blocking it effectively. His manner was an invitation.

Captain Hepburn poked at his mustache. "This Miss Ford is quite a friend of yours, isn't she?"

McBride scowled. "Meaning she'd lie for me?"

Hepburn's eyes steadied. "See here, mister, I don't like your trick of answering a question with another."

"I'm thinking 'way ahead of you," McBride said. He put his hands in his pockets and went over to the open ports. The Venetian blinds were drawn but music drifted back from the ballroom. They were playing soft and sweet again. "I don't blame you for looking me up. I'd do the same thing. But at least give me credit for being intelligent." He took a deep breath.

"A man smacks me in the mouth in front of half a hundred witnesses. An hour or so later he is found stabbed to death." He turned, spreading his hands, palms up. "I ask you."

Hepburn's glance gathered the others about him, making his next words theirs also. "It is our thought that perhaps he was not intended to be found. Perhaps his murderer was interrupted in the attempt to throw the body overboard."

McBride shrugged irritably. "The same thing applies, doesn't it?"

"Not quite. The absence of a body always complicates these matters a little. There is always that thing the courts call a reasonable doubt." He looked with a sort of clinical interest at Fessenden's mutilated back. "Like the case of poor Simmons," he said.

McBride licked his lips. This was getting pretty

deep, even for him. "Simmons was a lush. The chief steward told me so."

Hepburn's eyes flickered around. "Ah, so you asked, did you?"

"Of course. The little guy was my steward."

"Curiously enough," Hepburn said quietly, "we thought of that—after Fessenden was killed." He sighed. "We couldn't have thought of it before, worse luck."

There was a knock on the door. The chief officer let Rhys in. Rhys was a little out of breath. "He was in the bar, but the barman won't say for how long, nor that he couldn't have slipped out. There was quite a rush. He remembers serving Miss Ford, though."

"Thank you, mister." Hepburn sounded rather more disappointed than otherwise. His glance rested on McBride obliquely. "You're a private detective?"

McBride knew then that the radio clerk had talked. More than likely he had been investigated thoroughly before they'd sent Rhys after him. At any rate there was no good lying. "Yes," he said shortly.

"Care to tell us what your mission is aboard the *Honolulu Queen*, mister?"

"No," McBride said. He wouldn't have told them, even if it had had any bearing on Fessenden's death. "I'm sorry, but I couldn't do that."

For the first time the chief officer spoke. "There are ways of making him talk, sir."

"Try it," McBride invited. "I've been worked on

by tougher monkeys than you." He ripped open his shirt. There were scars all over his chest and upper abdomen. "Those aren't operations."

Captain Hepburn looked pained. "There is no question of physical persuasion, Mr. McBride. My First has just been reading too many magazines." He clasped his hands behind him and took a slow turn about the room. "Presumably you are a man of intelligence. You have said so yourself. Yet we find you spreading stories that you are the heir to two millions; that you are a temperamental writer and God knows what else. Already possessed of one cabin you rent another. A steward on your deck disappears. You have words with Fessenden and he is stabbed to death. Can you blame us for feeling that you are not quite as intelligent as you claim to be?"

"All right," McBride said, "I'm a screwball. Some guy—I think it was a man named Ingerman—once said I was the world's most unorthodox detective. But just the same, I did not kill Fessenden." He tried to remember the name for a maritime jail. "Throw me in the brig if you want to, but you can't prove I did kill him."

"And little Simmons?"

McBride's mouth tightened. "I know nothing about that."

Hepburn pounced. It was almost a physical act. "Then why do we find his successor parading up and down before your door, armed with one of your guns and refusing to say anything except 'I won't talk'?"

Hepburn didn't know it, but this last was a slip. McBride made a little prayer of thankfulness for Sweeney. "Oh, that," he said. "Hell, don't take it out on Sweeney. It was just my screwpot idea of a joke. He used to know me a long time ago. Always wanted to be a dick, so I let him be one. I told him the Communists were after me."

The captain tried a new attack. "How about your interest in Baron Itsuki and his in you?"

McBride cursed the radio man anew. For one who professedly hated Japs this guy had certainly spilled his guts.

"Well?" the captain prodded.

McBride looked embarrassed. "Well, I know it sounds silly, but lately it seems you can't turn around without hearing about Jap spies and one thing and another. I thought I'd check back on Itsuki just for fun. He must have seen me watching him and checked up on me." He spread his hands. "There it is. You'll have to take it or leave it."

The captain, the First, Rhys and the doctor all held a hurried consultation. The fifth member of the crew looked at McBride as though he might be a leper. McBride looked at the holes in Fessenden's back. He thought he would like to have a look at Fessenden's personal effects.

Hepburn faced him abruptly. "Mr. McBride, you are either a very smart man or a very foolish one. For the life of me I can't make up my mind which." He plucked at his mustache a little absently. "Suppose we put it this way. As our chief suspect, you will be more or less under constant surveillance. But if, as a detective, you are able to turn up a more logical suspect before we make Honolulu we shall remain silent about the apparently unrelated incidents pertaining to you personally. Otherwise we shall have no choice but to make a full and complete report to the Honolulu authorities when we turn you over to them."

McBride was honestly impressed. "That's fair enough, Skipper. That's a better break than I'd get in my own home town."

AND SUDDEN DEATH, XIV

BARON Ito Itsuki had around eighty dollars of McBride's money and the dice were still hot. McBride couldn't understand it, because the dice were his own. He had mentioned this to Itsuki several times in the last fifteen minutes. Both men were in their shirt sleeves, on the floor of the baron's sitting room, for even at one o'clock the night was warm, and there is no place like a carpet to shoot craps. The door to the lanai, or private veranda, was open, and the swish of the water far below was clearly audible.

McBride had been rather busy in the last few hours. The ship's company, shocked to wakefulness by the Fessenden tragedy, had helped to conceal some of his movements, but it was only a question of time before the radio desk would decipher some of his enigmatic messages to McGonigle and the almost as cautious replies.

Itsuki was shooting for a ten. "Did you kill Fessenden?"

"No," McBride said. "You did."

They sat there on their haunches for a long moment, regarding each other. "The maid too, I think," McBride said.

Itsuki grinned delightedly, his tiny mustache making that odd little V. McBride was reminded of the devil's horns. "Proof?" Itsuki said. The dice in his small fist rattled an instant before he rolled them. He sevened out.

"Before coming to America," McBride said, "you were attached to your London embassy. Either you finished your work there or things got a little too hot for you. After your departure some of your activities may have come to light."

Itsuki smiled. "You say *may* have come to light. There is some doubt, then?"

"About that," McBride nodded gloomily. "About Fessenden, no. A man I know was fortunate enough to find remnants of cablegrams and one thing and another among Fessenden's discarded papers. The hotel no longer burns its waste paper. They save it up and sell it to you Japanese. Funny, isn't it?"

"Isn't it?" Itsuki said.

McBride was watching the bedroom door, because he had discovered that Itsuki had a valet and it was possible the valet was beyond the door. "Fessenden, unfortunately, was not a trained agent. He just happened to be on the spot and they used him."

Itsuki made little disparaging sounds with his mouth. "To follow me?"

"To follow you," McBride agreed. He stood up. "I see you have moved the chenille throw-rug from in front of the divan. That's one of the things I came up to see you about. I thought that possibly there would be a wet spot on the carpet."

Itsuki too stood up. He was inches shorter than McBride. "And if there is a wet spot, my friend?"

"You can't wash blood out," McBride said.

"No," Itsuki said. His face was meditative. Presently he moved over to the console table against the wall and poured himself a drink from the thermos. Quite suddenly the lights went out. "Good-by, my friend." It was like a whisper from the lanai. Then the door slammed and there was no sound at all.

McBride moved unhurriedly to the wall switch, snapped it back on. He then opened the passage door and yelled, "Man overboard!" at the top of his lungs. Next he picked up the thermos jug and banged himself on top of the head with it. It was only after he had done all these things that he lay down and arranged himself as though he had fallen.

Faintly, from a dozen different points, his cry was taken up. The great ship vibrated as she went into reverse, and overhead was the pound of running feet. No one came out of the bedroom. The first man through the passage door was a steward. McBride, groaning, raised himself to an elbow. He had no wish to undergo heroic first aid.

The steward bent over him. "What happened? Was it in here?"

McBride waved feebly toward the lanai door. "The baron. Suicide!" He watched the man fling open the closed door and go out on the veranda. Magically the sitting room filled with people and McBride became quite a hero for a while. It was only after Captain Hepburn and Fourth Officer Rhys cleared the room of all save the doctor and McBride that they really got down to business. Rhys must get very tired, McBride thought. He seems to be everywhere. McBride was beginning to dislike Rhys a little.

The doctor was applying packs to the lump on McBride's head, first hot, then cold. "It's a wonder the thermos didn't break," he said.

McBride agreed with him. The way his head felt, the thermos could have been an anvil. Presently he pushed the doctor away and joined Hepburn and Rhys on the lanai. The white-painted rail was five pipes tall. On the second from the bottom the paint was scuffed a little. On the top rail, quite plain in the collected moisture of the night air, was the imprint of two small hands.

McBride sighed. "A nice little guy," he said. "I kind of liked him."

Rhys cursed. "I believe you deliberately let him get away!"

"Hold your tongue, mister," Captain Hepburn said.

They watched the beams of the great searchlight scan the crawling waters far behind. There were two powerboats out there. Their lights were like little winking jewels against the night. Motionless except for a slight roll the *Honolulu Queen* lay waiting for the return of her offspring.

After a long, long time Hepburn broke the silence. "Signal them in, mister." He sighed. "That's two I've lost this trip. A bad record."

Rhys went away. Hepburn and McBride waited till

the boats were hoisted up to the davits before they went inside. The *Queen* took up her interrupted journey. "You know," Hepburn said, staring very hard at McBride, "it's an odd thing but I have the same thought my Fourth expressed a little while ago."

McBride's "Have you?" was noncommittal. His was a somewhat peculiar psychology. He did not actually condone criminality, but he did understand it. At times he had been forced to do things not strictly within the law himself, and his liking for a man was not influenced either by ethics or the lack of them. A proven rascal, so long as he played fair with McBride, personally, was a right guy. Thus, in a measure, he felt no guilt whatever for permitting Itsuki to choose his own end. The little baron had committed, or was responsible for, murder. He was now dead. The law could have done no more.

Rhys came back, saluted Hepburn very smartly and turned antagonistic eyes on McBride. The doctor excused himself, pleading an imminent visit by the stork to a lady down on C deck. "A fine business," he said. "This is the third this year. I might as well be in the obstetric ward at the County." He went out, slamming the door.

Rhys said, "We have the valet, sir. He was caught hiding in a trunk room."

"Very good, mister." Hepburn sat down heavily. His index finger worried his mustache, but it was purely habit. He had no interest in it. "You'd better tell us a little more about it, Mr. McBride. For a man who apparently knew nothing a short time ago you've certainly accomplished a great deal." He sighed. "Of a sort."

"It was his neck or mine," McBride said. "I couldn't afford to be tied up in Honolulu while they were proving me innocent." He helped himself to one of Itsuki's cigarettes, lit it and exhaled a great cloud of smoke. "For the actual business of nailing Itsuki to the cross I did exactly what you did in my case—what any detective would have done. I looked for the motive. On the surface, Fessenden was nothing more than he seemed. Hell, I didn't even know he was a lord until after Rhys told me. But it was a cinch he wasn't killed as he was, and where he was, for the purpose of robbery. Any other motive, at least any other than the one ascribed to me, would have had roots somewhere in his past. I just got in touch with a friend of mine and he was lucky enough to get the breaks. Fessenden had been assigned to tail Itsuki, possibly to get something it was believed Itsuki had. The latter, I think."

"What was it?"

McBride made a gesture of impatience. "How do I know? Ask the British Intelligence, or Counter-espionage, or whatever you call them. All I know is that Fessenden must have tried prowling the baron's suite. He was a fumbler and got caught at it.

Rhys had a bright idea. "Then whatever he was after must still be here!"

"Sure," McBride said. It wasn't, though. Half an hour's intensive search brought absolutely nothing incriminating to light. Nothing, that is, that either Captain Hepburn or Rhys recognized as having any bearing on the case. The .32 revolver they found in among the valet's clothing was just a gun. McBride was convinced that it was the gun used to kill the maid at the Chelsea Arms. For one thing, it had been fired twice. The empty shells were still in the chamber. McBride did not mention the maid.

"But see here," Rhys protested, "we have only your word for all this! You mean you just came up here and accused Itsuki over a game of dice?"

"He won eighty bucks," McBride said aggrievedly. He had thought about retrieving the money, now that the baron would no longer have need of it, but discarded the idea as being unsportsmanlike. He kicked the chenille throw-rug into a ball. On the carpet beneath was a ruffled, faintly damp patch, darkening toward the center. "I don't think Itsuki himself would have done it this way. Probably the valet. But the little guy knew it was a showdown in either case. Operating under the guise of a diplomatic attaché, practically immune to prosecution as a spy, his exposure would nonetheless cause a tremendous scandal. It will anyway, but Itsuki won't be here to reap the consequences." McBride's brows drew down in thought. "Somewhere I read that it's a Jap's idea of honor to kill himself if he fails. Funny, isn't it?"

Rhys did not think it was funny. "I still think you let him do it!" He looked at Hepburn. "By God, sir, we'll get the truth of the matter from the valet!"

They went down to Deck D, but they did not get the truth of the matter from the valet. He had hanged himself. With his belt.

AND SUDDEN DEATH, XV

McBride was taking a brisk turn around the promenade of B deck the following morning as a prelude to lunch. He had breakfasted simply but quite charmingly on what Sweeney had left of the bottle of rye, and while this wasn't much, it and the unaccustomed exercise were together producing a remarkable appetite. McBride was in excellent spirits. He was wearing gray flannels, a lighter gray shirt, a darker gray tie. His dark skin and hair and eyes contrasted well with these and he felt that he made quite a striking picture, reminiscent of those excellent black-and-whites which used to illustrate the E. Phillips Oppenheim serials in the *Post*.

He felt that he might as well make a striking picture, because everybody aboard knew by this time that he was a private detective anyway. The ship's bulletin, constrained to quell the incipient riot caused by last night's events, had published all available data, and, despite Rhys, had given McBride whatever credit was due. People he didn't know from Adam's off ox were bowing to him. He was a celebrity.

Presently, having done the mile prescribed by the health faddists, and incidentally the first he had actually walked in perhaps ten years, he sank exhausted into the deck chair labeled with his name. The rug-covered figure in the chair adjoining turned out to be

Miss Ford. McBride was agreeably surprised. "Hello, hon!" He examined her critically. "You look sort of white around the gills."

"I feel white," she confessed. There were shadows under her eyes. She pushed the rug free of her face and sat up a little straighter. "Been having a nice time?"

He flushed. "So you've been watching me!"

Her smile was faintly cynical. "Why not? Everybody else is."

"Can I help it?" he demanded angrily. "You think I like this break you're crazy."

Miss Ford was lazily amused. "It's all right, darling. You never were one to hide his light under a bushel anyway."

He scowled at her. "My light, no. My business, yes. You never heard me spout off about a case yet until it was in the bag." He fixed her with a resentful eye. "Did you?"

"Except to—her," Miss Ford said.

McBride was furious. "Damn it to hell, why bring that up? I told you it was over. I meant it." He gnawed at his knuckles. "Hell, I'd practically forgotten her!"

Kay reached out a hand and laid it on his knee. It was a good hand, long and slim and fine. It belonged, somehow, with the rest of her. Impulsively he covered it with one of his own. "Let's not fight, kitten."

"All right, Rex."

"The fact of the matter is," he said after a while, "I'd about decided to ask you for a little help." He watched her covertly to see how she would take this. If it was bothering her because he had once spilled his guts to Sheila Mason, he would do the same for her. Not all of it, of course, but enough to satisfy her. Besides, he really needed her. "All this publicity is going to make it a little hard for me to get around."

Miss Ford was not as impressed as she should have been. That was the trouble with her. She had a million-dollar mind that was hard as hell to fool. "What are you up to now, Rex?"

"There you go," he complained bitterly. "Always looking for something that isn't there." He stood up. "All right, I'll get Sweeney to do it."

Miss Ford crossed her slim ankles. "What is it you want me to do, Rex?"

He was genuinely embarrassed now. "Well, with Fessenden gone, it's——" He broke off to stare very hard at a passing oil tanker. It was a Japanese boat. "What I'm trying to say, Kay, is that maybe you'd just as soon sit at some other table."

She nodded. "I know that's only part of what you want to tell me, Rex, but just the same its thoughtful of you. He was a good man, Fessenden. Seeing his chair vacant, or someone else in it——" She got up swiftly and crossed to the rail.

McBride followed her. "Then it's all right for me to fix it?"

"Of course. Anywhere you like." As he was turning away she put out a detaining hand. "You've left out something, Rex. What is it that you want me to do?"

He avoided her eyes. "I want you to cultivate Sybil Nordstrom. I'll introduce you later."

"She's the platinum personality at your table?"

"Unh-hunh."

Miss Ford was frankly amused. "The alternative being that you will have Sweeney do it?" She laughed throatily. "Rex, sometimes you amaze me. You flatter me too, comparing my charms with Sweeney's. I don't think I can stand it."

He scowled. "Then you won't?"

"Oh no, I didn't say that." She thumbed her nose daintily. "Run along, darling. Mama will cultivate that blond Jezebel rather than have you do it. Mama will simply love it."

Cursing her, McBride stalked down the promenade. It was very hard being a celebrity after the spanking just administered by Miss Ford. Down in the main foyer he arranged for a new table in the dining salon. This was not so difficult as it would have been had the *Queen* been carrying a capacity load. He gave no reasons for the desired change, though he had several. In the first place, he was quite sure by this time that he did not like Rhys. The fourth officer's antagonism was an annoyance, and McBride had discovered by somewhat devious means that the cause of it was Sybil Nordstrom's interest in himself. Rhys was jealous. An additional and unexpected factor was Rhys' relationship to Captain Hepburn. He was the skipper's kid brother-in-law. All in all it looked like a good bet to divorce himself from Rhys' table. The sand-and-gravel Carmichaels were a nuisance anyway.

McBride compromised on a table for two, so situated that it would be perfectly natural to pass his former place on the way down the long room. After that he returned to the foyer and the purser's office, where he bargained for at least a partial refund of the money expended on the cabin-class stateroom. The recent turn of events had necessitated a change in his plans regarding Teal and Fenner. He was no longer operating under cover; he was out in the open. Upon reaching Honolulu the task of tailing Sybil Nordstrom would be much more difficult than keeping track of her aboard ship. Being alone, the job would require a twenty-four-hour shift, obviously impossible if continued for any length of time. The hazard of losing her could be lessened for McBride if he let part of the burden fall on Teal, Fenner and the O'Connor girl. Their interest was as great as his. There were three of them. Consequently, should he, McBride, lose the quarry, he stood an excellent chance of picking her up again through one or all of the others. He would simply have to postpone his vengeance for little Simmon's death until a more opportune moment. He was unsuccessful in getting his money back. Sighing, he repaired to the bar.

As usual his cheerful mood was succeeded by a fit of black depression. He was sick of lying and cheating and chiseling. For a time he even wished he were a plumber. In this racket you were supposed to violate all the codes of ethics except one. You were hired to do a job and you did it. At the moment this did not seem a very noble thing. He thought once about telling Vickers and the whole Monolith Corporation to go to hell, but he couldn't very well do that, either. It would be like welshing on a bet.

A page boy came in with a radiogram from McGonigle. McGonigle was jubilant. "Nice going, boy!" the message said in part. This was in response to McBride's lengthy gram of the night before and apparently the *Tribune* had benefited to the extent of an exclusive. In McGonigle's mind, and in all save McBride's and possibly Sybil Nordstrom's, the great Jap Spy case was closed. It had no bearing on the Nels Nordstrom case. For that matter, McBride wasn't at all sure that his own judgment wasn't warped a little.

Baron Ito Itsuki, together with his valet, had lived in the same apartment house as Sybil Nordstrom. All right, that could be pure coincidence. The Chelsea Arms was open to the public. Then take the maid. She was doing a keyholing job for Monolith. Itsuki, being a spy, would naturally be alert for any suspicious actions on the part of those around him. Possibly the maid had tried branching out; say she discovered something damaging to Itsuki and tried to put the squeeze on him. So he had caught her and exercised a little persuasion. Witness her broken fingers. Under duress, what had she told him? Nothing about McBride, certainly. She hadn't known about McBride. But suppose she had cracked about Vickers? Suppose that in some manner Itsuki had got wind of McBride through the Monolith Corporation? Could be, McBride decided. That would account for the search of his court apartment. McBride snapped his fingers, remembering something.

By telephone he got in touch with Captain Hepburn. After that he went in search of Kay Ford. She was still where he had left her on the promenade of B deck. "Look, hon, this is a hell of a thing to ask you to do just before lunch, but I want you to take a look at a dead guy."

Her blue eyes darkened with apprehension. "Another? I mean, has someone else been——?"

"No," he said. "This is Itsuki's valet."

They descended to the cold-storage vaults below the water line. Rhys was waiting for them. He nodded distantly to McBride, thawed a little for Miss Ford. "This is hardly the place for a lady."

McBride lost his temper. "Then the sooner we get it over with, the sooner I can get the lady out of here!"

Rhys compressed his lips. "Am I supposed to know the purpose of this visit?"

"If you are," McBride said nastily, "get your brother-in-law to tell you."

"Rex!" Miss Ford admonished him.

"I don't care!" McBride snarled. "This guy keeps getting in my hair." He glared at Rhys. "I'll tell you one thing, pal, we're not down here working up an appetite. Let's go."

Rhys led the way to a steel door a little apart from the other steel doors marked: "Meat Storage No. 1," and so on. There was a combination dial and he twisted this, flinging the door wide. The unmistakable smell of a morgue was in the icy dank air. Miss Ford's face was as white as the rubberized sheet McBride pulled down. "Well?"

She nodded an affirmative. McBride's fingers bit into her arm as she would have gone on. He didn't want Rhys to know the exact circumstances under which she had first seen the valet. He pushed her out of the vault and tossed a curt "Thank you" at the fourth officer. They went up to the smoking-room bar. Over Martinis McBride said quietly, "You're sure?"

"Yes, Rex. He is the man I saw outside your place."

McBride lapsed into gloomy silence. If he had needed any further proof of Itsuki's interest in him he now had it. The baron's valet was the one who had wrecked the Hollywood place. Presumably it was either he or the baron himself who had later searched McBride's cabin aboard the *Honolulu Queen*. The thing that was not so clear was the reason for the search. The possible, indeed the only, motive that McBride could put a finger on was the theory that Itsuki may have feared himself to be the object of the portended espionage. He may have thought it possible that McBride was other than just a private operative; perhaps a government man. This surmise was borne out to a certain extent by the radio clerk's observation that Itsuki seemed more relieved than otherwise upon establishing McBride's exact status. In other words he had no particular fear of a private dick. But one of Uncle Sam's agents was something else again.

In all this McBride had the uncomfortable feeling that there was something wrong with the picture. It worried him, like an incomplete puzzle, nagging him, asking to be explained. The killing of the maid, for instance. Obviously necessary to the baron's well-being, why had it been accomplished the way it had? A gun is a noisy thing. If she were a captive why hadn't they simply slit her throat? The answer to this seemed to be that someone had lost his head, or that she had been on the point of escaping.

Again, there was the matter of Fessenden. They hadn't used a gun this time, but they had committed the murder in the baron's own suite. And in this case they hadn't been so lucky in covering up as with the maid. The discovery of Fessenden's body before it could be tossed over the side was the vital issue in uncovering the whole business. McBride was becoming more and more impressed with the fact that Baron Ito Itsuki was a little too thoughtful, a little too clever, to have done these kills himself. He had simply been cursed with an over-zealous retainer.

Miss Ford's voice impinged itself on McBride's consciousness. "If I'm boring you, darling——"

He glared at her. "Can't you see I'm thinking?"

"About what, my pet?"

"About Itsuki, if you must know. He's still chasing himself around in my mind and it bothers me."

Miss Ford's very lovely eyes widened a trifle. "But Itsuki is dead!"

"Sure," McBride admitted. "Deader than seven hundred dollars." He emptied his glass. "Just the same he was a smart little hombre and it was just his misfortune to have a guy working for him that wasn't so smart. What was Fessenden after? Why didn't we find it in either Itsuki's things, or the valet's?" McBride answered his own question. "I'll tell you why. Because after Fessenden's kill, after the body was discovered, Itsuki was smart enough to know an investigation might lead back to him. He was prepared for it; prepared to do exactly what he did. I could tell by the way he acted, but if this weren't enough, there's the valet's hiding and subsequent suicide. Itsuki told him what to do when and if such and such a thing occurred."

Miss Ford touched the back of her hand to McBride's cheek. "You're not drunk, are you, darling? Or feverish? Itsuki simply carried whatever it was over the side with him."

"Did he?" McBride didn't sound convinced. In fact he wasn't convinced, because of a couple of things that he knew about Baron Itsuki. There was the baron's nocturnal visit to Sybil Nordstrom's suite. There was also the utter certainty that Itsuki had known Sybil Nordstrom prior to embarkation. If Itsuki had known her it was probable the valet had too, and the valet, bungling as the search of McBride's apartment had been, couldn't have missed seeing her photo with those of Teal, Fenner and Company. So the baron knew that McBride was after the lovely Sybil. Had he known why? Had he been aware that Fenner and Teal and Chalice O'Connor were also aboard?

To this last McBride mentally said no. But he believed the baron had warned Mrs. Nordstrom about him, McBride. Her attempt to explain Itsuki's visit to her suite was proof positive of this. She wished to cover up more than a passing acquaintance with the Japanese, to convey the impression that he was just a casual invitee to a party where others were present. McBride had discounted this in the first place. Now he was quite sure that the baron had had no part in the chase after Nels Nordstrom's two million dollars. Ergo, Sybil Nordstrom was something more than the bait intended to spring the trap on her husband. Indeed, McBride was rapidly coming to believe that the whole thing was just a wild-goose chase. She wasn't going to meet her husband at all. She was accompanying a Japanese spy for a purpose, and to a destination, unknown—at least to one Rex McBride. This was the thing he had been trying to pin down, the thing that had been worrying him all along. He and Teal and the rest of them had been suckered into following a decoy that wasn't a decoy at all, but a live duck.

"Rex," Miss Ford said, "you're cursing terribly."

"Who wouldn't?" he demanded. "Good Christ Almighty, who's going to pay me—the government?"

AND SUDDEN DEATH, XVI

SYBIL Nordstrom did not come down for lunch. This left only Rhys and the Carmichaels and the lady who wrote for the love pulps at Rhys' table. McBride and Kay Ford, at their own private little table, were quite conscious of being discussed, and McBride, though not a lip reader, could have told you almost verbatim what was being said. The captain's table, because it was the captain's table, suffered little from the absence of Miss Ford, Lord Fessenden and Baron Ito Itsuki. It was full up again. Captain Hepburn seemed depressed, speaking only when spoken to, spending a great deal of energy poking at his mustache.

Over against the far wall Chalice O'Connor ate in solitude. Obviously this was because she wanted to be alone, not because there weren't plenty of takers for the chair opposite. McBride decided he'd have to do something about Chalice. She was too nice a girl, etc., etc. Also, though a little young, she was good-looking as hell. Redheads had so far been a closed book to him. Besides, he was a little sorry for her, being, like himself, misled by a red herring that stank to high heaven. He ate ravenously.

Miss Ford regarded him with patent disfavor. "You've got a vile temper," she observed.

McBride admitted this readily. In extenuation he offered: "But it doesn't last long, hon."

"You are secretive, too," she said.

"Am I, hon?"

"And a braggart, also," she continued. "An egoist of the first water, a preyer upon women, a selfish creature with no morals and little or no heart."

He was offended. "No good points?"

"I'm trying to make up my mind," she said. She wrinkled her very nice nose. "There must be something about you, but I'm darned if I can think what it is."

He chewed rhythmically. "My new shirt, perhaps?"

She thought this over. "No, it can't be that," she decided. "I liked you before I even saw it."

"Ah, then you do like me?"

"I'm afraid so."

He wiped his mouth. "This is very nice of you, Miss Ford. May I reciprocate and say that I like you too?"

Her blue eyes darkened. "It's really no more than that with you, is it, Rex?"

He looked at her. "So now we're turning serious, eh?" He helped himself deliberately to another chop. "What is it you want of me, Kay? Marriage, a home, kiddie kars in the drive?" He made a bitter mouth. "I'm no good, hon. You know it and I know it. Why don't you pick out a guy like Fessenden and make him happy?"

She shivered, thinking of Fessenden. McBride watched the play of light and shadow on her face. "Christ, Kay, with your looks and your mind, not a woman in the world could pass you in the stretch."

She was intelligent enough not to argue this. There wasn't any argument. She knew what she had. "It isn't any of those things, Rex. Not exactly, anyway. I'd just like to go along with you, sort of a partner. You've got the makings of a very great man, McBride."

His face was a sardonic mask. "Aren't we the Mutual Admiration Society?" He leaned forward a little, holding her eyes with his. "Listen, Kay, once and for all I'll tell you the God's truth. If I let myself go I could be nuts about you. That's what I'm afraid of. I'd be nuts about you and then you'd find out that I'm not the guy you think I am, and we'd bust it up and I'd probably cut my throat." He looked away. "I've been hurt once. I don't like it."

Her voice was low. "Thank you, Rex."

He stared at her. "For what?"

"Just for being you, I guess." She leaned back, smiling. "You wouldn't know it, of course, but you just said one of the very nicest things a man ever said to a woman."

He stood up violently. "A fine business!"

"A lovely business," she agreed. "Where are you off to now, darling?"

He scowled. "Well, if you must know, and just to show you I didn't mean a word I said, I'm going up to see Mrs. Nordstrom. And maybe," he added darkly, "maybe we'll even get drunk together."

"That will be nice," Miss Ford said. She lit her own cigarette, blew the match out. "Better leave your valuables with the purser, though."

He swore. "Now listen, if you think for one minute——"

"And make her buy the liquor," Miss Ford said.

McBride strode angrily away. Going up in the elevator he wondered what he should say to Mrs. Nordstrom. Maybe, he thought hopefully, she's dead. He was very displeased with Mrs. Nordstrom, and with Vickers of the Monolith Corporation, and McGonigle and all the rest of them. The idea, dragging him, McBride, way out here in the middle of the Pacific Ocean with a fairy story about two million dollars. Already he was figuring some way to increase his expenditures so he wouldn't have to refund any of the ten grand to Vickers.

He got out of the elevator on A deck and crossed the ultra-luxurious foyer to the short passage leading to No. 8. These lanai suites were the most expensive aboard the *Honolulu Queen*. There were only twelve of them and they lay directly beneath the bridge and the officers' quarters. Each had its own private veranda, separated from the next by a solid partition. The sitting rooms and bedrooms were furnished like bridal suites. McBride knew all this from his momentous call on Baron Itsuki the night before. What he did not know was how Sybil Nordstrom could afford it, unless Itsuki had stood the tariff. And if this last were true, and Itsuki had need of clandestine meetings with Sybil, why hadn't he taken an adjoining suite instead of one on the other passage, with a double row of trunk rooms intervening?

McBride pressed the buzzer beside the door of Number 8. He had to wait quite a little while before there was any response at all. Then the door opened a bare two inches. "I didn't ring," Mrs. Nordstrom said.

McBride put his foot against the door. "And I'm not the stewardess, darling."

Mrs. Nordstrom caught her breath. "Oh, I'm sorry. I've been asleep."

"I missed you," McBride said gallantly. "I thought you might be ill." He still kept his foot against the door. "May I come in?"

She hesitated. "I don't know. Perhaps for a little while. You'll have to wait till I get something on, though."

He said he was always glad to wait while a lady got something on. The door closed. A man and a woman passed him, disappearing into Suite 2. He felt like a callow youth, caught loitering outside a burlesque stage door. When presently Mrs Nordstrom admitted him, however, he was glad he had waited.

She was wearing pale yellow lounging pajamas, heavily embroidered in silver, and there were high-heeled golden sandals on her narrow feet. He was pleased to note that she had put on stockings, because he was one of those to whom a leg without a stocking is a definite disappointment. The satin of the pajamas was so sheer he could see where the stockings ended, above the knee. Around her throat was a silken scarf, also pale yellow, and her platinum hair was coiled low at the base of her neck. He thought that any other woman would have been colorless in the ensemble. Sybil Nordstrom was vital, a living study in gold and silver.

"Well, do you like me?"

His eyes glowed. "I couldn't miss, Beautiful." He leaned toward her, magnetized by the challenge in her sea-green eyes. Her mouth was a scarlet invitation. Presently he freed himself. "That was something, Beautiful, no fooling."

There was a luncheon tray on the low table beside the divan. There was also a ship's newspaper. "Been ill, Sybil?"

"A little," she confessed. She moved over to a cabinet against the inside wall and got out a bottle and glasses. "Drink?"

He nodded. The liquor was rye. "Is this an accident, or did you know I liked rye?"

"I like it myself," she said. She tossed hers off neat, immediately poured another. McBride's eyes admired her. He had the feeling that she was under a tremendous strain of some sort. The lanai door was open, as was the bedroom. It was as though she had anticipated his interest and was showing him she had nothing to conceal. She set her empty glass down. "So you're a great detective."

He bowed mockingly. "The name is Holmes, Beautiful." He frowned. "If Itsuki was a friend of yours I'm sorry. I kind of liked the little guy myself. It was just one of those things."

She shrugged. "He was no friend of mine."

McBride had the distinct impression that this was the truth. He couldn't have told you how he knew; certainly this woman before him was not unaccustomed to dissembling; still, there it was. If he had ever sensed active dislike, not to say actual hate, he sensed it now in Mrs. Nordstrom's "He was no friend of mine."

She had another quick one. McBride said, "Hey, if this is going to be a race let me get in on it!" He poured a water glass half full. "Now you can help yourself, baby. I've got mine."

She looked at him. "You always get yours, don't you?"

He measured her. "Meaning what, Beautiful?"

"Meaning you're a detective. A Los Angeles detective." She indicated the open newspaper. "Nobody could have been around as long as you have without knowing who I am."

"All right, then I do know who you are. So what?"

She moved aimlessly about the sitting room and he sipped rye, watching her expectantly. She's not common, he thought. Not so dumb, either. Bright sun, streaming in through the open lanai door, silhouetted her figure. The sheer yellow satin was only a golden high light. Beautiful, he thought, beautiful as hell. The rye was beginning to work on him a little.

She laughed. It was a brittle, tinkling sound, like the glass wind-bells the Japanese novelty stores used to sell. "Are you following me, McBride?"

He sucked in his breath. Well, he thought, we're certainly out in the open and that's a fact. He chuckled, quite convincingly, he thought. "Why should I be, darling?"

She turned to face him. "Let's not haggle, McBride. Suppose that what you believe to be true is actually true. Then what?"

He drank thirstily. "I don't know what you mean."

She wasn't laughing now. Her eyes were cloudy with emotion, like the swirl of water above the propellers, before it bubbles up and spreads into the wake. "Show me one other reason for your being aboard and I'll believe you."

Damn it, he thought, maybe Itsuki didn't tell her! Maybe she's just guessing. But at that she's guessing pretty close. He tried to put a lot of sincerity into his tone. "Look, Sybil, maybe you know as much about me as I do about you. If you do, you'll know that I busted a case in which a woman was involved. I was crazy about her. I just had to get out of town for a while, is all."

She shrugged. "It doesn't matter a great deal." She poured herself another stiffish drink. "Tell me about yourself, Rex McBride. Are the stories one hears about private detectives true?"

"Sure," he said, "we're all scum. We'd murder our own grandmothers for a dime." He grinned at her. "Anybody you'd like knocked off—cheap?"

For just an instant she was startled, as though the idea hadn't occurred to her before but might not be such a bad idea at that. Then her eyes once more became unfathomable. "I could be very nice to you,

McBride. And if it's money you're after I'll be able, in a little while, to bid higher than anyone else could. Want to think it over?"

"Baby," he said warmly, "I don't have to think it over. You've sold a bill of goods."

Her green eyes probed him. "But this other woman? The one you turned up?"

"You don't have to worry about that," McBride said. "If she'd made an offer like yours maybe I wouldn't have."

She smiled at him. "You really are a heel, aren't you, darling?"

He caught her to him. "You're damned right I am. That's what you want, isn't it?" Releasing her presently he saw that the silken scarf had fallen away from her throat a little. In the firm white flesh was the blue imprint of fingers.

AND SUDDEN DEATH, XVII

McBride came down the passage, stepping high, like a man climbing stairs. He had a decided list to starboard. The door to his cabin was wide open and the lights were going full blast. He spread his arms wide so that he wouldn't fall through the doorway until these various phenomena were explained to his personal satisfaction. The room was thick with cigar smoke and perhaps this was why McBride saw two Sweeneys, sprawled out in two chairs, reading two magazines.

"You're drunk," Sweeney observed critically. "Drunk as a boiled owl."

McBride squinted his eyes. "What's the idea?"

"How should I know?" Sweeney shrugged. "It ain't me that's drunk."

"Cause why?" McBride demanded triumphantly. "Cause you drank up all my liquor last night, that's why!" He peered intently at Sweeney's feet, which were in the middle of the bed. "Anyway, that's not what I mean."

Sweeney put down the magazine with a sigh. "Oh, you want to know what I'm doing in your cabin? Why, it's on account of by leaving the door open, and the one to my cubby, I can hear the buzzer any time it rings. It's just like I was right at my own desk."

"Not to me it ain't," McBride said. He corrected

himself. "Isn't." He stepped carefully over an imaginary foot-high threshold and made his unsteady way to the bed. He fell on it.

"Jesus, you're drunk," Sweeney said.

"I am not. Jus' sleepy."

"And you got lipstick all over you too."

McBride burrowed deeper into the pillows. "What color?"

"What color?" Sweeney demanded indignantly. "He asks me what color. Why, lipstick is red, you dimwit!"

McBride was too tired to go into the fine nuances of lipstick shadings. "Okay, pal, run some water in the bath, hunh?"

"You mean you're going out again?"

"Gotta eat," McBride mumbled. "Gotta keep up strength." He slept. He dreamed hazily of Fenner and Teal, who, it now seemed, were twin devils prodding McBride with fiery pitchforks toward a flaming caldron of molten metal. This scene, much to his relief, was supplanted by a more intimate one with Sybil Nordstrom, who was offering him her lips and a bushel basket full of twenty-dollar gold pieces at the same time. The only trouble with this picture was that Nels Nordstrom, her husband, was standing in the doorway behind her, pointing a gun as big as a cannon at McBride's stomach. A ghostly Baron Ito Itsuki applauded from the side lines.

The awakening was terrific. Unaware that he had been undressed McBride thought at first that his clothes were on fire. Then he saw that he was stark naked in a bathtub filled with what felt like white-hot lava. Sweeney beamed down on him. "How's it, pal? That'll fix you right up."

McBride tried to get up, but motion only seemed to make the water hotter. Cursing, he sat there and watched himself turn tomato-red. Steam and alcohol fumes floated up from him in great clouds. "You, Sweeney!" he yelled. "What's the idea?"

Sweeney materialized in the bathroom door. "It's on account of I once worked in a Turkish bath," he explained cheerily. "Believe me, pal, I've fixed up plenty lushes in my time. Pul-lenty."

"I'm not a lush!" McBride yelled.

"Well, maybe not, pal, maybe not. Only it seems like three out of the four times I've seen you, you cer'nly ain't been no Carrie Nation."

McBride, now accustomed to being boiled in oil, relaxed. He slid down until the water lapped his chin. "Those were accidents."

"I'll bet."

"Well, they were." McBride was moved to self-pity. "Nobody knows what a detective has to go through in the performance of his duty."

"I do," Sweeney asserted. "You think the skipper didn't give me hell last night, you're crazy. But I wouldn't talk," he added proudly. "I told him I wouldn't talk and I didn't, neither. I said, 'Gwan, torture me,' I said, 'but you nor nobody else is gonna make me talk!' "

"You were adamant," McBride said.

Sweeney regarded him suspiciously. "I was what?"

"Firm," McBride said. "Like a rock."

"You're damn' right I was!" Sweeney grinned. He reached down suddenly and opened the drain. His right hand gave the shower valve a twist and McBride yelled bloody murder as the cold water hit him. "Good God, do you have to kill a guy?"

"This is war," Sweeney said sententiously. "War on the Demon Rum, like the lady said. She said I should sober you up."

McBride glared at him. "What lady?"

Sweeney smirked. "Not the one you been gettin' drunk with. The lady." He stressed the last word. "Miss Ford." His eyes closed rapturously. "Hair like Midnight, eyes like stars, a figger like——"

McBride was toweling himself tenderly, afraid the skin would come off. "Like Venus?" he suggested.

Sweeney made disparaging sounds. "Hell, that Venus! I seen a statue of her once, out at Exposition Park, it was, and by God she couldn't get to first base nowadays." His two hands described the voluptuous curves of Venus. "To heavy in the—now—hips."

"I see," McBride said gravely. He repaired to the bedroom and began getting dressed. It must have been all of ten minutes later when Sweeney returned from a trip down the passage. He was preoccupied. "I wonder who got her arms?"

McBride was deep in his plans for the evening. "Whose arms?"

"Why, Venus's, of course!"

"Christ!"

"Well," Sweeney demanded aggrievedly, "do you know?"

"No."

"Then you got no right to laugh at me," Sweeney scowled. He uncorked a half-pint flask, tilted it to his mouth, put it back in his pocket without offering it to McBride. "A hell of a dick you are!" He followed the slug with two of his violet breathlets. "Sometimes I don't know what I see in you."

"I'll check the bet," McBride said. "I don't know either." He went out and down the passage and knocked on Miss Ford's door. She opened it almost at once. "Hello, Rex." She was wearing white tonight, very simple, very expensive. By contrast her hair was, even as the poetic Sweeney had said, like midnight, and her eyes, while not exactly like stars perhaps, were so darkly blue that you thought of stars, or maybe violets at dusk.

Something, possibly a belated appreciation of his rare good fortune in knowing her, brought a sudden lump into McBride's throat. To mask this strictly sentimental reaction he glowered at her. "So you've been spying on me!"

She was complacent. "Of course."

"Well, I don't like it, see? I won't have it!"

She ignored this. "You look very nice, darling. Nice and clean. Did Sweeney wash itty bitty Rex's ears?"

His description of Sweeney was biased but vivid.

"Not that I blame him entirely. You told him to do it."

Miss Ford was shocked. "You mean you didn't *want* to get clean again?"

He avoided her eyes. "Well, hell, I told you I was going to get stinko, didn't I? Besides," he added, "I was working."

"Oh?"

"Well, I was. Believe me, I'm going to search that babe's room tonight if its the last thing I do."

She widened her eyes. "Tonight! What were you doing all afternoon?"

His grin was a trifle sheepish. "Trying to get her drunk enough so she'd go to sleep." His eyes glowed at the memory. "Christ!"

"Perhaps she has hollow legs," Miss Ford suggested.

"I thought of that," McBride said. He narrowed his eyes in pretended puzzlement. "They didn't feel hollow, though. They felt——"

"Rex!"

"There you go," he complained. "You're just like Sweeney. You've no idea what a dick has to endure in the line of duty."

"I can guess," Miss Ford said drily. She took his arm and they descended to the dining salon. This being the last night out, dinner was quite an affair. The big room throbbed with the music of a full string orchestra and the hum of voices was like surf on a rocky beach. At the captain's table Hepburn presided, very magnificent in gold braid. All the rest of them were there, the Second and Third, almost as magnificent; the Chief, oddly enough not a Scotsman; and the purser who looked like a bank's vice-president. Rhys, the Fourth, had filled the gap in his own table, and only the First Officer was absent. The wind had risen during the afternoon and the *Queen* was pitching a little. McBride supposed the First had to be up on the bridge. He was glad that someone was up there. The inside of his stomach felt as though it had been sandpapered.

Rhys had the freshly scrubbed look of the very young. He smiled mechanically as McBride and Kay paused beside the table, but his eyes were still resentful of McBride. Mrs. Carmichael looked a little dowdy, McBride thought, her husband pontifical. Miss Smythe, the writer, was quite vivacious after the manner of a schoolteacher on vacation. The man who had taken McBride's place was reminiscent of the traveling-salesman legend. Sybil Nordstrom's sea-green eyes appraised Miss Ford's gown.

Between Rhys and McBride introductions were performed all around and Kay had already turned away when Mrs. Nordstrom touched McBride's arm. He bent over her. She was angry and trying not to show it. "Playing the field, darling?"

He shrugged. "I don't like Rhys. You didn't come all morning and I had to do something, didn't I?"

"I don't like such stiff competition."

He whispered in her ear. "For you, Beautiful, there is no competition."

Her eyes remained hard. "Then I'll see you right after dinner?"

It was a blow, but he took it in his stride. "Right after dinner," he promised. Cursing under his breath he followed Miss Ford across the crowded room to their little table against the far wall. He was glum all through the meal, saying little, eating without his customary appetite.

Presently Miss Ford, remarking his preoccupation, said casually, "Bad news, Rex?"

"In a way," he admitted. "Short of knocking her out I can't prowl her room when I'm with her. She can drink me cross-eyed."

Miss Ford considered this. "I assume she has commanded your presence after dinner?"

"That's right." He flushed uncomfortably. "It isn't what you think, not on my part, at least. If you'll remember, I told you this morning I wanted you to cultivate her. The main idea was to be sure she was taken care of while I went through her things." He frowned. "It's a little late for that now."

"We could reverse the procedure," Kay offered. "You entertain the lady while I do the prowling."

He thought about this for a moment. So far as he could see, Kay would be in no particular danger. From past experience he knew her to be capable enough, and if he was as good as he thought he was he certainly should be able to keep Sybil Nordstrom interested for the length of time necessary. "It's an idea," he said. He looked at her. "You'll have to be careful."

"Of course."

"I don't mean just about leaving traces, either. I don't want you hurt."

"There's a possibility of that?"

"I dont' know," McBride confessed. "I don't think so or I wouldn't let you go." He made a bitter mouth. "Just the same, there's a hell of a lot of things going on that I don't know about. Anything could happen."

"What arrangements have you made with Mrs. Nordstrom, Rex?"

"Apparently she needs me for something. I don't know just what yet. She's hinting at money in large quantities and this might mean her husband." He shrugged. "Maybe she wants me to kill him for her. I wouldn't know."

"But you don't really think that, do you?"

He stared out over the room. "Could be. On the other hand, maybe it's just a stall. Maybe she's pretending to cross her husband so that she can cross me. Maybe she isn't going to meet him at all, but is using that as a herring to pull me off something else. She thinks all private dicks can be bought."

Miss Ford smiled. "Isn't that your own favorite line, Rex?"

His brows drew down. "Well, hell, that's what the public thinks, isn't it? Why should I go around championing a lost cause? Let 'em think it and to hell with them."

She laid a hand on his. "It's tough pretending to be a heel all the time, isn't it?"

"I am a heel."

"Of course you are, darling." She accepted her coffee from the steward, waited till the man had gone on. "What am I supposed to look for?"

McBride took a deep drag on his cigar. "Something that might give us an idea where Nels Nordstrom is. Failing that, something that would prove she knows where he is." His dark eyes got a curiously intent look. "But mainly the business concerns the Baron Ito Itsuki."

Kay caught her breath. "Rex, are you sober?"

"They knew each other," he said stubbornly. "And the little guy was smart, I tell you. I can see him committing suicide, all right, but I'm damned if I can see him tossing away the reason for the whole thing. Whatever he had was intended to do his country some good. He wouldn't take it to the bottom of the ocean with him."

"Meaning that she has it? That rather implies that she is a traitor to her own race."

McBride nodded gloomily. "Not only her race but her country. As I see it, Fessenden's angle wasn't the only one. Itsuki did a job in England and moved on. How do we know he didn't do the same thing with us?"

Miss Ford stood up. "I'll do my best, Rex."

"I know you will, hon." He grinned at her. "Get a passkey from Sweeney. He'll give it to you. He thinks you're a lady."

Under cover of her handkerchief Miss Ford thumbed her nose at him. "I am a lady." She went away.

McBride lingered over his cigar and coffee, watching the people around him, watching especially Sybil Nordstrom. She had chosen to wear yellow and black tonight, only the yellow wasn't exactly yellow either. It was more of an amber, with the same quality of rich transparency. The bodice was black, backless, but cut very high in front, with a sort of choker effect at the throat. Very convenient, McBride thought, remembering the purplish marks of fingers. Her hair was pale gold plate. Now that Miss Ford had left she was easily the most beautiful woman in the salon. And probably, he thought, the most unscrupulous. He wondered why unscrupulous women invariably chose him to pull their chestnuts out of the fire. Perhaps they sensed a certain affinity of spirit. Perhaps he looked more sinister than he thought he did. Or maybe they just took him for a sucker. He winced, recalling the way another woman had made a sucker out of him. The fact that she was in jail did nothing whatever to bolster his ego.

Presently, seeing Mrs. Nordstrom preparing to leave, he too got up and made his way unhurriedly down the room. She was refusing the escort of the man who looked like a traveling salesman. McBride held her jacket for her. "Ummm, you smell beautiful, Beautiful. What is it?"

"Passionette," she said shortly.

They went out to the foyer. "Sore about something, Beautiful?"

She gave him a level stare. There were violet shadows under her eyes. "I saw the way you looked at that woman."

"Who, Miss Ford?" He laughed. "How did I look at her?"

"Skip it," she said. "I want a drink."

He shrugged. "Okay, baby." They went up to the intimate little bar off the night-club ballroom. It was still quite early for the crowd and the orchestra was whanging away at something, mostly for their own amusement, certainly not for McBride's. He would have resented being told he was old-fashioned, but about music he was. He couldn't work up a good sentimental jag any more. All swing did for him was make him irritable. His mood showed in the way he drank. After the third or fourth he put both elbows on the bar and glared at Mrs. Nordstrom's reflection in the mirror. "I can find plenty of more interesting people to sulk with than you, babe. Want me to?"

The stem of her glass snapped. "No."

"Then why don't you come out of it?" His eyes held hers steadily. "If I hadn't wanted to play it your way I wouldn't be here, would I?"

The barkeep came down the bar to see about the broken glass. Mrs. Nordstrom ordered a refill. McBride refused. "Would I?" he persisted.

She turned her sea-green eyes full on him. "What would you do for, say, fifty thousand dollars, Rex?"

"Show me the guy," he said.

She emptied her glass. "Maybe I will, at that, darling. When I get to know you a little better."

In the mirror McBride saw Sweeney come through the arch from the supper club. Sweeney shouldn't have been there. His place was on B deck. McBride slid off the stool and went over. "What's wrong, pal?"

Sweeney gulped. "The lady," he said. "Something's happened to her."

Miss Ford was lying in her own cabin, even as Fessenden had lain in his, though in her case she was fully dressed and there was no blood in evidence. The ship's doctor and a woman in white who might have been a nurse or a stewardess were in attendance on her. Her eyes were closed and her breath came in erratic little gasps, sometimes with the intervals so long in between that you thought the next one was never coming.

McBride's face felt as stiff as cardboard and he too was having trouble with his breathing. Anger burned in him so terribly that it was like constricting fingers on his throat. Sweeney shuffled his feet in the doorway. Perhaps it was the cessation of this, the only sound, that made McBride turn. Fourth Officer Rhys was just coming in. His eyes took in the scene swiftly, centered on McBride. "I insist on an immediate explanation, mister. Too many things are——"

"Get out," McBride said.

Rhys took two swift steps forward and caught the doctor's arm. "Is she able to talk yet?"

"Get out," McBride said again.

Rhys swiveled on a heel. His eyes were hot. "I'm damned if I will, mister!"

McBride hit him. It did not seem to be a hard blow, but Rhys' head snapped back and his knees went rubbery. McBride caught him before he fell, lifted him easily and carried him out into the passage. He then went back inside the room and closed the door. He was breathing carefully, as though afraid of disturbing Miss Ford.

The doctor looked at him. "That was neat, Mr. McBride. Neat but not very politic, I think."

"The hell with that. What's wrong with her?"

"Concussion. How bad I can't say just yet. I've given her a slight heart stimulant."

"There's nothing more you can do?"

"Short of somewhat heroic measures, no. I think it better to let her come out of it quietly."

"Then you can get out too. You and the lady."

The doctor took off his glasses, polished them, put them back on again. "As you wish. Come along, Miss Weems." At the door he turned. "If you don't mind a suggestion, Mr. McBride, you could do with a drink." He and Miss Weems went out.

McBride stood there for a little while, quite still. Then, unhurriedly, he turned the key in the lock and went over and knelt beside the bed. "Come on, Kay, I'm pulling for you." That was all he said. He did not ask God for help, because it seemed to him that this was his own personal problem. He couldn't expect God to repair the damage that a guy named Rex McBride had caused. Gradually the stiffness went out of his shoulders and he buried his face against the cool whiteness of her gown.

It might have been hours later, or only minutes,

when he felt her hand on his head. "Hello, darling."

He straightened. She was still very pale, but she was smiling a little. "Hello, Kay," he said. Their hands met, but neither said anything more for a while. Presently she stirred and looked around her. Her eyes formed a question.

"I don't know yet," McBride said. "They must have carried you down, I guess." He touched her cheek with a gentleness foreign to him. "Feel like talking about it?"

She wet her lips. "I would like a little water, I think."

"Of course." He got up and poured a little from the thermos, held the glass to her lips while she drank. She lay back against the pillows. "It wasn't her, Rex?"

"It couldn't have been, hon. I was with her every minute." He was surprised at the steadiness of his own voice.

"Then who?"

He looked down at his right hand. It was shaking. "I've an idea, hon. I'll take care of it."

She winced as though at a sudden pain. "I wish you wouldn't, Rex." She shivered. "I have a feeling that—that there are forces at work here that neither of us understand. It's a rather horrible feeling, Rex. I wish——"

"I'll take care of it, hon." He went to the phone. "Will you ask the doctor to come up here again, please?" When he turned he was smiling. "I just want to be sure you're not going to have a relapse."

She closed her eyes. "I—I didn't find anything, Rex."

"Forget it."

She shuddered. "He must have been there all the time. In the wardrobe."

"Who?" McBride said sharply. Instantly sorry he came and knelt beside her again. "Forget it, hon. I'll take care of everything."

She went on as though she hadn't heard him. "I'd covered the cabin, all the logical places, and there was nothing. Then I opened the gown wardrobe and something came out from behind the dresses and hit me. That's all I remember."

"You're sure this was inside the cabin?"

"Of course. That's why I thought you ought to know. Whoever found me there—It will look pretty bad for us, won't it?"

"You weren't found there," McBride said shortly. "You were outside in the passage." He went to the door in answer to a knock. It was the doctor again. McBride looked at him. "I'm sorry, Doc. Sorry if I was rough."

"I like roughnecks, Mr. McBride. Especially when they can hit like you do." Apparently the doctor was not too fond of Rhys himself. He went over to the bed. "So you've decided to wake up, have you?"

Kay smiled crookedly. "Wasn't I supposed to?"

He harrumphed professionally. "How do you feel?"

"I've got a head like a barrel," she confessed.

"You've got a good head of hair, anyway," he said.

"Lucky for you." He turned and pointed his pince-nez at McBride. "The captain wants to see you, mister."

"Later."

The doctor shook his head. "Now. Shipmasters are funny that way. When they say now they don't mean tomorrow."

"The hell with him."

The doctor gnawed at his nether lip. "There's nothing further you can do here. Miss Ford will be quite all right. My word on it." He appealed to Kay. "Tell him not to be a fool. Hepburn is in a position to hang him if he likes."

She propped herself on an elbow. "Please, Rex."

"All right!" he said savagely. He turned at the door to point a finger at the surgeon's chest. "Just the same, if anything else happens to her I'll come back and cut your heart out!"

"I'll even lend you the knife," the doctor said gravely. McBride went out. Sweeney was hovering in the passage. "Look," McBride said, "you still got that gun of mine?"

"Sure, boss."

"Then lay off the liquor and keep an eye on Miss Ford's door. I mean keep an eye on it."

Sweeney was indignant. "Now look, pal, you're not blaming what happened on me. It wasn't even on my deck." He leered ingratiatingly. "Now if you was to take me into your confidence, even a teeny-weeny little bit——"

"I'd end up with an anchor around my neck," McBride said. He entered his own room, got the smaller of his two guns and shoved it in the waistband of his trousers. He thought once about disregarding the captain's message until after he'd taken up one or two little matters with George Teal and Saul Fenner. Then he decided they could wait, because it was a cinch they couldn't get away without committing suicide. He climbed the stairs to A deck, then to the boat deck and finally those leading to the officers' quarters abaft the bridge.

Captain Hepburn was not in a pleasant mood. His eyes resented McBride, though he kept his manner carefully polite. He sat behind his massive desk, an old man but not an incompetent one, a monarch absolute aboard the *Honolulu Queen*. Rhys, beside the door through which McBride had just come, was nursing a discolored and swollen jaw.

"Mr. McBride," Hepburn said, "I have tried to be fair with you, have I not? In the matter of certain peculiar, not to say tragic, circumstances aboard my ship, I have exercised the utmost leniency. Agree with me?"

"Sure."

"I have recognized your privilege, so far as possible, of keeping your affairs to yourself. But you have not kept them to yourself, mister. You continue to endanger the lives of others in my charge. I can not tolerate such a condition any longer."

McBride looked at him. "I don't get it."

Hepburn colored angrily. "Sir, my fourth officer—"

"Your brother-in-law."

"Very well, my brother-in-law. I understand from him that Miss Ford identified Itsuki's valet. This leads to the inevitable conclusion that she was implicated prior to the exposure of Itsuki. Also it ties into the theory that there was more to the case than you led us to believe."

"Does it?" McBride said. His eyes looked sleepy, but behind them his mind was doing flip-flops. His respect for Hepburn grew. Turning suddenly on Rhys he pointed a dramatic finger. "Tell the truth, Rhys. Did you hear Miss Ford say one word while we were in that vault? Did you?"

"She nodded," Rhys said sullenly.

McBride whirled on Hepburn. "You see? Obviously your fourth officer has been prejudiced all along. You yourself have noticed it. Who shall say what a woman's nod may mean, especially under such circumstances?"

Hepburn compressed his lips. "But you cannot deny that you did take her down to the vault for the purpose of getting an identification."

"I'm not even trying to," McBride said. "All I ask is that we stick to facts; facts uncolored by an overimaginative and slightly jealous young man who happens to be your brother-in-law."

Rhys let out a yelp at this. Hepburn silenced him. "Did I understand you aright, Mr. McBride? You said jealous?"

"He's got a hero complex," McBride said.

"You're a goddam liar!" Rhys yelled.

McBride passed this off with a shrug. His manner said that he and Captain Hepburn were men of the world, not the sort to take offense at the unprovoked outbursts of youth. He even lit a cigarette to show how calm he was. He became very respectful. "So far, sir, nothing has occurred that hasn't had a full and reasonable explanation. I did take Miss Ford down to the vault. If you remember, I called you and asked permission to view the remains. Miss Ford accompanied me because she is something of an authority on the Japanese and I was curious to know whether she thought him the low-caste valet he pretended to be."

"But what of the attack on her this evening?"

"I'm sure I don't know, Captain. Miss Ford herself has recovered sufficiently to say that she didn't see her assailant either. Possibly it was some moron. I suggest than an investigation along those lines would give your fourth officer something to do. Besides," he added significantly, "annoying guests."

Hepburn stared very hard at Rhys. "I'll have a word with you alone, mister. After Mr. McBride leaves." He returned his attention to McBride. "I am making a full report to the Honolulu police. They will probably wish to question you."

"Certainly," McBride said.

"And if I may say so, sir, I will be very glad when you leave my ship."

"That makes two of us," McBride said. "I always wondered why I never took an ocean voyage. It must have been a hunch." He went out. He was sweating slightly under the arms.

The *Queen* had run into a rain squall, one of those tropical downpours that last but a short while but shed a lot of water while in action. McBride was drenched by the time he had crossed the narrow stretch of open deck between the officers' quarters and the gymnasium. He took shelter under one of the canvas-covered boats and lit a soggy cigarette. The gymnasium showed no lights; the tennis courts and deck sports areas, open to the weather, naturally were deserted. McBride reveled in the rain, the sense of being utterly alone. He even abandoned the meager protection of the boat presently and stood at the rail, staring out to sea. Far below him the swish of the waves against the ship's plates was a reflection of the turmoil that was in his mind. Rain drummed on his bare head, cooling, stimulating.

After a while he shook himself and went below. In the B deck passage leading to his own cabin he ran into Sweeney.

"Jesus, you're wet!" Sweeney said.

McBride pretended to be greatly surprised. "Now how did that happen?" He looked down at himself. "Sweeney, old pal, you've got the makings of a great detective. I certainly am wet and you spotted it almost instantly."

"Aw!" Sweeney said. He helped himself to a violet.

McBride eyed him severely. "So you've been drinking again!" He licked his lips. "Got any more of that scorpion spit?"

Sweeney said that he hadn't. He said, "And I wouldn't give you some if I had any." The breathlet crunched between his teeth. "On account of you never take me into your——"

"Confidence?" McBride assumed the air of an arch-conspirator. "Sweeney, old pal, that's just what I am going to do." He looked around him furtively. The passage was empty of all save Sweeney and himself. "How is Miss Ford?"

"She's asleep. The doc gave her something."

McBride sucked in his breath. "He leave any of it lying around?"

"Unh-unh."

McBride sighed. "Too bad."

"You mean you want a Mickey Finn yourself?"

"Well," McBride said, "it isn't for me exactly. It's for a friend of mine who just can't get to sleep." He peered hopefully into Sweeney's eyes. "You wouldn't be able to sneak a dram or two from the dispensary, would you?"

"Not me, pal. I got troubles enough."

McBride sighed again, heavily this time. "I was afraid you wouldn't." He unlocked his door. "All right, then, there's nothing left but out-and-out debauchery. Get me a quart of rye and six raw eggs."

Sweeney was suspicious of a rib. "What's the eggs for?"

"To armor-plate my intestines, pal. I'm going to put an inner lining in my stomach." He looked sadly at Sweeney. "You've no idea what us dicks have to go through."

"Nuts. I bet you're gonna throw a bust with that blonde babe up on A deck."

"Well, I'm taking you into my confidence, aren't I? What more do you want?"

"Some of the rye," Sweeney said. He went down the passage to his cubbyhole and presently McBride could hear him using the telephone. McBride went into his own room and began shedding his wet clothes. He was almost fully dressed again when Sweeney appeared. "I brung some red pepper, too," Sweeney said.

"What's that for?"

"To take the curse off the eggs."

McBride went about the serious business of putting a false bottom in his stomach. Ten minutes or so later, armed with the quart of rye and an ingratiating smile, he tapped on Mrs. Nordstrom's door.

Her voice sifted fuzzily through the panel. "Who is it?"

"Look," McBride said, "gifts."

"I don't want any. Go away."

McBride leaned on the door. "I'll scream, darling."

The lock clicked and the door came open. "You're drunk."

"Sure. Wouldn't you like to be?" He held up the bottle. "Look, Beautiful, I'm sorry I had to leave you flat. I've been catching hell from the skipper and one thing and another. But the night's still young."

She stepped back and he went in. She was still wearing the amber and black. Her green eyes were alive with suspicion. "That woman was in my cabin!"

McBride ceased his efforts at opening the bottle. An idea he had begun to entertain in the last few hours was practically made a certainty by the hurled accusation. He knew Kay Ford. Told to not leave any traces, she wouldn't. There was only one other explanation. "Was she?" he said easily. "How do you know?"

Mrs. Nordstrom masked, or tried to mask, her momentary confusion by an assumed petulance. "Here, give me that bottle!"

McBride held it behind his back. "No, seriously, how can you be sure she was actually inside? I understood she was found in the passage."

"Isn't that enough?"

He shrugged. "Well, maybe."

"You sent her!"

"Did I, Beautiful?" He held the bottle to the light, admiring the color. "Do you think it's like me to cut any more in on the gravy than I have to? Ever occur to you that she might be a little jealous; a trifle sore because you took me away from her on the last night out? Besides," he added casually, "you don't know that she was actually inside. Or do you?"

Mrs. Nordstrom must have sensed where he was leading her. "Well, no——"

He followed up his advantage. "Teal and Fenner are aboard."

She stared at him with a sort of horror. "How do you know that?"

"I get around," he said easily. He smiled. "Believe me now, babe, when I say I'm on your side?"

She sat down suddenly, as if all the strength had gone out of her legs. "Jackals!"

"Worse than that," he agreed.

"The lousy rats!"

"Oh, I don't know," he said. "You can't blame them for wanting a slice of all this money you're talking about."

She reached for the bottle. "You're a devil."

"But a very nice devil to have around, Beautiful."

She drank thirstily. Apparently she had had a slight edge on when McBride arrived and for this he was properly grateful. "Where are they?"

"Teal and Fenner? Down in Cabin Class 411." He gave her their assumed names. It would have been perfectly all right with him if she had gone down and shot them both. It would save him the trouble of doing it personally, later. He couldn't have told you why, at the moment, he had refrained from mentioning Chalice O'Connor, daughter of Frank O'Connor, who was still in Folsom because of Nels Nordstrom. Perhaps it was because he was a little sorry for her. It was possible that she was not a party to the Simmons kill. Perhaps it was because he didn't think it necessary. He rarely did unnecessary things.

Mrs. Nordstrom permitted two tears to leak from her lovely eyes. "Oh, darling, I'm so alone!"

"Not any more, you aren't," he said. He bent over her. "Don't worry about Fenner and Teal, Beautiful. We'll take care of them." He poured himself a drink.

After that the bottle of rye became, like an hourglass, an accurate gauge of the lapse of time. McBride's stomach stood up surprisingly well. He was no more than pleasantly lit when Mrs. Nordstrom passed out. He sat there for a little while, watching her slide soddenly, bonelessly out of the chair. After a while he got up and carried her into the bedroom and went about the business of searching her person. At another time, under other circumstances, it would have been a pleasure. He did not find it so now. He simply did what he had to do, as a surgeon performs a necessary operation. Presently he went out of the suite, closing the passage door but leaving it unlocked. His eyes were tired and very, very disillusioned.

AND SUDDEN DEATH, XIX

THEY slid in past Diamond Head at ten in the morning, flags flying, bands playing, the entire ship's company lining the rails. McBride, who had done a little forced-draft research amongst the various travel agencies' literature, found himself quite familiar with the immediate scene, as though he had been there before. The green of the sea did change to blue, then deepen into indigo, even as the books had said. Palm-fringed Honolulu climbed the mountains as described and spread into the narrow green valleys between them. Waikiki, with its Royal Hawaiian and half-dozen other beach hotels, was a riot of color, and the *Honolulu Queen* was even now being surrounded by a jittery fleet of launches, outriggers, speedboats and half-pint sea sleds.

McBride, impressed and trying not to show it, watched others around him, less self-conscious, tossing coins over the side for the edification and profit of wildly imploring native divers. I will come back some time, he thought. When I can be a kid like the rest of them. Maybe with Kay, just the two of us. He was feeling very old this morning, very sentimental. Band music always made him sad, somehow.

Miss Ford, beside him at the rail of B deck, and quite stunning in crisp white linen, was apparently none the worse for her experience of the night before.

She flipped a quarter from her purse, watched a lithe brown body flash in pursuit of it. "Love me, Rex?"

"I think so," he said cautiously. Over Punchbowl Hill was a rainbow, remnant of a morning shower. He thought this might be a good omen. A couple of tugs puffed importantly alongside and took the *Queen* in tow. They went in between Sand Island and Fort Armstrong, up into the harbor proper and past Aloha Tower. The smell of pineapples from the canneries was heavy and sweet. "You don't mind the Mauna Loa?"

Kay shrugged. "The Royal Hawaiian is only a name to me. A hotel is a hotel, anywhere in the world."

"You understand why I had to make it the Mauna Loa?"

She looked at him. "You're curiously apologetic this morning, Rex. Of course I understand. Mrs. Nordstrom is going there."

"That's right, hon. All I want you to do is see that she gets there as advertised." He moved his shoulders impatiently. "They've got a show in New York called *Hellzapoppin*. If I'm not mistaken this case is going to be much like it, only not quite so funny."

"Why, Rex?"

"Because I lit two or three fuses last night. They ought to touch something off pretty soon now." He glowered as a third tug pulled alongside and a bunch of official-looking uniforms came aboard. "Watch your step, hon. I'll be seeing you around." He pushed through the crowd on the promenade and entered the foyer, so that Rhys wouldn't have to look so hard for him.

What followed was oddly unreal, as though he were dreaming it. In the delegation which finally converged on him were Rhys, Captain Hepburn, a reporter, a news photographer, and a man in whites who turned out to be a detective-lieutenant of the Honolulu police. Outside, the din was terrific. The shrill tooting of the tugs fought valiantly against the deep bass of the *Queen's* bellow, and all three of the ship's bands blasted a challenge at the welcoming bands ashore. The photographer coyly draped a lei of ginger flowers around McBride's neck, and then, before he could remove it, stepped back and shot two pictures. The flashes almost blinded him. He felt like the prize winner at a horse show.

The detective-lieutenant's name turned out to be Stone. He was the most polite cop McBride had ever met. "May I see your identification, Mr. McBride?"

McBride produced his license. Stone gave it a quick glance, returned it. "And your business in the Islands, Mr. McBride?"

"Do I have to have any?" McBride asked.

Rhys cursed. "You see, Lieutenant? He persists in answering one question with another."

Stone said crisply, "It strikes me, mister, that you're taking the wrong attitude with Mr. McBride." He pulled a sheaf of papers from his pocket. "In this transcript of your radio report to us I find nothing to Mr. McBride's discredit. As a matter of fact, I think we are all indebted to him." He passed the transcript to McBride. "Essentially correct?"

McBride ran through the typed report. It seemed incredible that there was no mention of Sybil Nordstrom, Teal, Fenner or the O'Connor girl. He had been living with them in his mind for so long that he could scarcely believe he hadn't dropped a stitch somewhere. He decided he must be a very smart man indeed. He grinned at Hepburn. "My compliments, Captain. For a man as prejudiced as you have been, this is a singularly unprejudiced report."

Hepburn flushed. "I merely recounted the facts, sir, not my suspicions." He glared at Lieutenant Stone. "Just the same, if you could have been aboard——"

Stone nodded. "These things always look worse when they're right under your nose." He tapped the report. "A steward commits suicide. An Englishman is murdered and his murderers do away with themselves. There is an unexplained attack on a Miss Kay Ford. All happening on the same voyage, one cannot blame you for assuming a connection that possibly did not exist." He looked at McBride. "I'm sure Mr. McBride understands this."

"No hard feelings on my part," McBride said.

Stone smiled. "Where will you be stopping?"

"The Mauna Loa."

"Then I think that is all," Stone said pleasantly. "We shall probably get in touch with you later. The inquest, you know." He turned away.

McBride let out his breath slowly. He still couldn't

believe it. Stone, about to enter the elevator with Hepburn and Rhys, thought of something else. He came back. "We of the Islands like to be courteous to our guests, Mr. McBride. We expect the same courtesy in return."

McBride was suddenly aware of the man's potentialities. This copper was no fool. Polite, yes. Not a guy to go off half-cocked. But was he really dismissing Rex McBride with a casual wave of the hand? He was like hell. McBride shook the proffered hand. "You're the smoothest cop I've ever met, Lieutenant."

"You get smooth in the Islands," Stone said. "Not," he added, "that there aren't smoothies elsewhere." He returned to the waiting elevator.

The reporter had a newspaper. "Thought you'd like to see this, Mr. McBride. Flown over from the Mainland." The sheet was McGonigle's *Tribune*. McBride and Baron Itsuki had been relegated to Page 2. The powers in Europe and the Far East were already allocating, on paper, various parts of the Western Hemisphere, as though the conquest were an established fact.

"Christ," McBride said.

"Unh-hunh," the reporter said. "The commentators don't seem to realize it, but maybe what Baron Itsuki was carrying had a bearing. Has it occurred to you ——" He broke off, shrugging. "There's a hell of a lot of Japanese in Hawaii, Mr. McBride."

McBride was suddenly quite sick. Trying to locate a lousy two million dollars, he was tinkering with something that was far too big for him; too big for any one man. "Thanks, pal, thanks for calling something to my attention." He went out on deck. He was still wearing the lei of ginger flowers. Discovering this presently he was about to take it off when it occurred to him that he would probably be more conspicuous without it than with it.

The sleekly white *Honolulu Queen* was already in dock and brown-skinned giggling flower girls were all over the ship. A guy without a lei was practically the same as a guy without his pants. Sweetly insistent music was everywhere, and joyous shouts of welcome, and the shrill laughter of women.

McBride, binoculars to his eyes, watched the gangways from above. There was little or no delay in debarkation; no fussing over passports, because this was still the United States. Probably in the whole ship's company there wouldn't be more than half a dozen who weren't American citizens. He was not quite sure what would happen to George Teal and Saul Fenner, because they were on the passenger list under assumed names. They might be stopped. But when he saw them at the head of the after gangway, saw the immigration officers pass them without question, he left the rail and descended rather hurriedly.

His own clearance was expedited by the okay of Lieutenant Stone. McBride squeezed through the crush on the pier, trying to keep far enough behind Teal and Fenner not to be spotted, yet close enough so he wouldn't lose them. Teal was carrying his own bags. Fenner had none. It was at the intersection of

Queen Street and Mauna Kea that the two men separated. McBride had been afraid of this. It was one of those things you hoped wouldn't happen but usually did. Both Teal and Fenner had been in stir long enough to learn the ropes. Knowing they were under observation they would at least take ordinary precautions to shake a possible tail.

The enormously fat Fenner paused to light a cigar, finally turning to the right down Queen Street. McBride, suspecting that Fenner, on account of his size and because he would have to get his luggage some time, might be easier to pick up later, continued on across Queen in the wake of George Teal.

Teal was well-dressed, prosperous-looking. Perhaps two or three inches taller than McBride, though not so heavy, he had a quick, nervous stride that was difficult to judge. He carried the two bags easily, without effort. McBride tailed him across to Beretania Street and to the door of a very middle-class hotel called the Swanson House.

McBride did not go in for a while. But when Teal finally came out again, without the bags, McBride pushed through the doors and approached the desk. "Was that my friend Teal who just registered?"

The clerk was a washed-out blond kid. "No sir, that was Mr. Craven. Mr. George Craven."

McBride pretended to be greatly disappointed. "My mistake, I guess." He went back to the street. Teal was still using the same alias. McBride hoped that Fenner would be as obliging. He stood there for a little while, getting the feel of this strange city at the crossroads of the world. Around him was the oddest collection of humanity he ever expected to see. Primed for it by his study of the travel brochures he was nonetheless surprised to find Japanese, Chinese, Filipinos and Whites all mixed up in a sort of harmonious hodge-podge. The Beretania Street buses looked exactly like the buses at home.

Presently, deciding that the guy under the umbrella in the middle of the street must be a cop, McBride went over. The guy was a cop. He was Chinese. "Palace Square?" McBride said. "You catchum?"

"I catch," the cop said. He said it gravely and quite courteously. "King Street is three blocks that way." He nodded. "The one with the streetcar line. Palace Square will then be a matter of seven blocks to your left."

McBride retired in some confusion. He was almost run over by a Beretania Street bus marked: "Palace Square." The bus driver did not curse him. The cop did not laugh. McBride then and there resolved that some day he was going to make Honolulu his permanent home. This was Heaven. He got on the bus.

AND SUDDEN DEATH, XX

THE Federal building was of Spanish origin, or at least of Spanish architecture. It housed the post office, the customs service and, according to McBride's information, other United States departments. Studying the directory board in the lobby McBride chose what to him seemed the most suitable department and ascended the stairs. Up here on the second floor there were not so many people. McBride located the office he sought, took a deep breath and pushed the door open. There were several young men at desks behind the long mahogany counter. On McBride's entrance they all looked up, examined him briefly, then returned to their work. An older man appeared from somewhere farther down the room. He smiled on McBride. "May I help you?"

"I don't know," McBride said. "The name is McBride. I have some information about the Baron Itsuki affair."

A sort of stunned silence followed this announcement. The older man, the one who wished to be helpful, recovered first. "Pardon me just a moment, Mr. McBride." He went through an unmarked door, closing it after him. All the young men watched McBride covertly, as though he might be slightly off center. Presently the older man reappeared, lifted a flap in the counter and motioned McBride inside. "This way, please." He ushered McBride through the unmarked door. He himself did not come in.

The man at the broad desk had the brownest face, the whitest hair and the keenest gray eyes in the world. The eyes regarded McBride quizzically. "Good morning."

"What is this?" McBride demanded irritably. "You'd think I was a leper or something!"

"Oh, no," the brown man said. "We don't think you're a leper. We think you're slightly more dangerous than a leper." He massaged his chin. "Just what is your business with this department, Mr. McBride?"

"Well, for Christ's sake!" McBride said.

The brown man stood up and thrust a brown, pudgy hand across the desk. "I'm Cord, Mr. McBride. Have a chair?"

McBride ignored the hand. "The hell with you." From an inside pocket he produced a thick Manila envelope. He tossed this on the desk top. "I don't know what half of that stuff means. If you do, you can have it." He turned toward the door.

"Just a moment," Cord said. He had a short, thick body which you imagined was as brown as his face. He was wearing a suit of wrinkled tan pongee. "You can't get out till I'm ready anyway," he said calmly.

McBride thought that this was probably a fact. Shrugging, he crossed to the tall windows and stared gloomily down at Palace Square and the Territorial Capitol across the way. Behind him was the faint rustle of papers.

After a little while Cord said, "May I ask how these came into your possession, McBride?"

McBride did not turn. "You can ask."

There was a small silence. Again it was the white-haired man who broke it. His voice was curiously impelling. "You're not exactly accustomed to discipline, are you?"

"If you mean red tape, no."

Cord's chair creaked. "I gather that you are relinquishing this material at some personal cost to yourself."

"You're damned right I am!" McBride said savagely. He swung about to face his inquisitor. "I was hired to do a job and this is going to bust it higher than a kite. I knew that when I came up here, but I came anyway." He took a breath. "And what do I run into? A bunch of stuffed shirts like every other government bureau!"

"I see," Cord said gravely. "I see your point."

"The hell you do!" McBride yelled. "You and your kind let a Jap come into our home diamond and steal us blind. You let him walk right out again. And then you've got the nerve to criticize the way a poor dumb shamus does the job you should have done in the first place. Christ Almighty!"

"The bull in the china shop," Cord said.

McBride flushed angrily. "By God, I get results!"

"Damned if you don't," Cord agreed. Presently McBride saw that he was laughing quietly. "Care to tell me about it, McBride?"

McBride told him about it. He told him profanely

and at great length. Finishing, he found that his anger had strangely evaporated. He had the mildly masochistic glow of the martyr. "So there you have it. Go ahead and pick up the dame. Sweat her to death for all I care." He grinned sheepishly. "Maybe she wasn't going to meet her old man after all."

Cord looked at him. "You don't really believe that, do you?"

McBride said quite honestly that he didn't. "At one time I had my doubts, but since then several things have come up that indicate she's planning her moves way ahead. She's a smart baby, that one. On the surface it may not look like it, but she is."

"And by coming to me with these"—Cord stirred the sheaf of papers with a blunt brown forefinger—"you felt that you were risking how much? Say ten per cent of whatever Nordstrom has left?"

"You'll have me crying on your shoulder in a minute," McBride said. "Old Flag-waver McBride. What's two hundred grand to a patriot like me?"

Cord stripped the paper from a piece of gum, folded the stick neatly and put it in his mouth. He made a little airplane out of the wax paper and sailed it across the room. "Mr. McBride, you are a curious mixture of native intelligence and blockheaded, stubborn foolhardiness. Except for the one instance I have no complaint with your handling of the case. I suggest that you let things work themselves out as planned."

McBride stared. "Am I as smart as all that?"

"You'll probably have a little help," Cord said drily.

"Meantime I don't know of any better scheme than the present one." He touched the papers again. "At least we have these."

"Yeah," McBride said pessimistically, "whatever they are. Personally, I don't think the Japs could have figured them out either." He picked up his hat. "Well, I'll be seeing you around?"

"No doubt," Cord said.

McBride went out and descended to King Street, feeling that maybe the government had something in this guy Cord. He caught an openwork Waikiki streetcar and sat beside a little old lady in black alpaca. He felt swell. He was still wearing his lei of ginger flowers and he thought that if he only had a ukelele he would sing. The monkey-pod trees nodded to him as he went by, and the oleanders blushed, and all in all it was a very nice world indeed. He decided that he would kiss Miss Ford when he next saw her.

After a while they stopped the car and the conductor told McBride which was the Mauna Loa Hotel. He went up a long, palm-bordered drive, through acres and acres of gardens riotous with color. The sun was liquid gold. The tennis courts and putting greens, the broad reaches of lawn and the lanais of the small individual bungalows he passed were all alive with people. He felt a oneness with them, like a Boy Scout who has done his good deed for the day. He felt virtuous as hell.

He felt this way until he saw Miss Chalice O'Connor come out of one of the bungalows. The sight of her recalled events that had little to do with virtue. Not that she wasn't, physically at least, in tune with the rest of the scene. She was bareheaded and the sunshine made of her coppery hair a halo. Her clear brown eyes regarded him without surprise.

He took off his hat. "Hello, there!"

"Hello, Mr. McBride."

A little devil prompted his next observation. His warm eyes linked her with the obviously expensive luxury of the Mauna Loa. "You must have had a profitable trip."

She flushed. "I think we can stop pretending, Mr. McBride. You may not have known at the time my real reason for being in your cabin. You do now."

"Do I, hon?"

"Yes." She looked past him to where, beyond the row of tall royal palms, the pale blue stucco of the main hotel was like a jewel against the sea. Her small hands were clenched. "I hate her, and I hate her husband. Nothing you can do or say is going to stop me."

His voice was a caress. "Have I tried to stop you, hon? I could have, you know."

She nodded. "I know. I think that's—that's why I felt I had to talk to you." She caught her breath. "It—it isn't what you think, Mr. McBride. I don't care about the money. It's my father. Nels Nordstrom's full confession is the only thing that can get him out."

McBride made a bitter mouth. "You're in bad company, Chalice. Very bad. You'd better wash it up before it's too late."

"No."

Quite suddenly he felt very old and very wise and, curiously, gentle. Perhaps it was the climate, or the perfume of flowers, or just her youth. "Look, hon, I'm supposed to be a very tough guy. In fact I am a tough guy. I'm not like you say you are. I'm after Nels Nordstrom because it means money in my pocket." He stared out across the broad vista of gardens. "Just the same, I'd hate to see you hurt, Chalice. Take my word for it, you will be hurt if you don't quit now."

"You seemed—different, somehow. I thought we might——"

"Work together?" He laughed shortly. "Not so long as you are mixed up with Teal and Fenner." He watched her face. "They won't stop at murder, Chalice. In fact they haven't stopped at murder."

"That isn't true!"

He made his voice deliberately brutal. "Remember the steward that disappeared? How do you think Teal and Fenner knew enough to send you prowling my cabin for further information?"

She shivered. "You have no proof of what you're saying!"

"No," he said quietly. "No, hon, I have no proof. But believe me, I know. Fenner and Teal are going to die one of these days. You may too, if you don't get out from under."

He turned away. The enormously fat Saul Fenner was just turning in from the drive. McBride passed him without a word.

At the desk in the main lobby he found that the hotel's agent aboard ship had made all the necessary arrangements. His luggage had already arrived and was in his room. Miss Kay Ford, it appeared, had the room adjoining. Judicious inquiry placed Sybil Nordstrom on the floor above, but in the same wing. Saul Fenner was not registered, either under his own name or an alias.

Crossing the lobby toward the elevators McBride ran into none other than Miss Ford in person. They adjourned to the lanai overlooking Waikiki, and at a little table they had cocktails. Miss Ford was sporting a double lei of gardenias. "You look so romantic, darling, with that rope around your neck."

He grinned. "I feel like the winner of the Santa Anita handicap." He sipped his *daiquiri*. "Just the same, you don't have to call it a rope. Why remind me of unpleasant things?"

"Like being hung, you mean?" She regarded him with acute suspicion. "What have you been doing with yourself all morning?"

"I've been being a patriot."

"I'll bet."

"Well, I have," he insisted.

Her eyes darkened till they became even bluer than the sea. "Rex, there's so much about this case that you haven't told me. We are seeing tremendous changes in the world, and now with this Japanese spy business ——" She shivered. "Where are we going to end up?"

"Maybe they'll make me a colonel."

"Rex, I'm serious! It needs only something like this Itsuki incident to ignite us too."

"Forget it!" he said sharply. He was remembering what Cord had said: "Except for the one thing——" Cord hadn't approved letting Baron Itsuki escape punishment. McBride stood up. "What did you find out?"

"I followed her to the Japanese Consulate. She did not go in. There was a flower vendor outside and she stopped and bought some flowers of him. I think they exchanged something but I could not get close enough to be sure. After that she went to the *Dispatch* office and, I think, put an ad in the paper. From there we came here."

"She see you?"

"I'm sure she didn't."

McBride was relieved. "Thanks a lot, Kay."

She too got up. "What's next on the program, big chief?"

"For you, nothing." He held up a hand as she protested. "No, I mean it, hon. I can predict what's going to happen next almost as surely as though I had second sight. I don't know just how soon, but sometime in the very near future there's going to be murder and sudden death. I don't want you caught in the middle of it."

She was angry. "And how do you suppose that makes me feel?"

"I don't give a damn how you feel," he said callously, "just so I know you're not lying around somewhere with your throat cut. Go out and play golf. Go out and find yourself a native and learn to ride surfboards. Do anything you like, but keep out from under my feet." Abruptly he swung around and went inside and so to his room. It was funny that he never seemed to do the things he intended to do. He had been going to kiss Miss Ford the moment he saw her.

Unlocking his door he paused on the threshold. "Well, for Christ's sake!"

Sweeney nodded happily from the depths of the most comfortable chair. "Sure, Chief."

"How did you get here?"

"I jumped ship."

"Well by God you can just jump back again then!"

Sweeney was hurt. "Meaning you don't want me, Chief?"

"Meaning just that!"

Sweeney relaxed. "Well, that's tough, pal. On account of there ain't nothing you can do about it now. On account of the *Queen* has sailed." He closed his eyes. "She oughta be out of sight by this time."

AND SUDDEN DEATH, XXI

McBride was propped comfortably in the chaise longue in the angle formed by the corner windows of his room. He was naked, save for dressing robe and slippers, and he had a late afternoon edition of the *Honolulu Dispatch.* With the stub of a pencil which he moistened frequently he was checking off advertisements in the Personal column. He couldn't seem to find the right one. "Maggie, come home," didn't sound like it. Neither did: "To whom it may concern: My wife, Carlotta, having left my bed and board, I will no longer be responsible for her debts. Signed, Manuelo Rodriguez."

McBride's pencil hovered a long time over: "To-night, dearest. Silly," but he finally discarded that too. On the small table at his elbow a siphon, a quart bottle of rye and a bowl of ice cubes offered relief from his labors. He felt that he was entitled to a respite. He had been working very hard. He had telephoned the brown-skinned, white-haired Mr. Cord and told him about the flower vendor outside the Japanese Consulate. He had telephoned various agencies in town, trying to ascertain where Mr. Saul Fenner had had his luggage sent. Unfortunately, both of these enterprises had come to naught. By the time Mr. Cord's minions had arrived the flower vendor had departed. Mr. Saul Fenner and his luggage had apparently vanished into thin air. McBride felt rather bad about this. He disliked the thought of having to annoy Miss Chalice O'Connor. He swished a little of the liquor around in his mouth and once more attacked the classified ads. Under "Help Wanted, Male," he found the item he sought. The classification bolstered his opinion that Sybil Nordstrom was a very smart woman. The ad read: "N. Mauna Loa. S." It was possible, of course, that N and S meant North and South, and that the Mauna Loa was the extinct volcano. McBride didn't think so. He thought it would be very nice if Nels came to Sybil instead of the other way around.

He made a neat black border around the item with his pencil and then flung both pencil and paper to the floor. He began a serious onslaught on the bottle, hoping to get his before Sweeney reappeared. There was a knock on the door. "Come in," McBride said.

Sybil Nordstrom opened the door. "May I?"

McBride wondered how a woman, any woman, could carry so many complete changes around with her. Sybil was wearing a white knit suit and a floppy white felt hat. The wide brim shadowed her eyes, so that he was unable to tell whether she had come to kill or kiss him. "Sure," he said carelessly. "Sure, come on in, Beautiful."

She closed the door behind her, moved toward him. She did not come all the way. "I lost something last night."

He leered at her. "Your virtue, Beautiful?"

"I want it back."

"Your virtue?"

She tapped her foot impatiently. When he refused to take his eyes off her face she opened her bag quite frankly and took out a gun. "I said I want it back, McBride."

He wondered how big a hole her first slug would make. Not very big, he thought. Then he remembered that in some spots it didn't take much to kill you. He emptied his glass. "I don't blame you a bit for wanting it back, babe. But why come to me?"

"Because you took it."

He shook his head. "Sorry, Beautiful, wrong number."

Her face was very white. The rouge stood out on it like blood on alabaster. "You're a liar, McBride. I know you took it. You're the only one who could have."

"Aren't you forgetting Teal and Fenner?"

Sweeney came out of the bathroom behind her. For a man who looked so clumsy he moved with surprising ease. His right hand, flattened, came around and chopped down on her gun wrist. The gun thudded to the carpet. Whirling like a cat she aimed a vicious kick at his stomach. He caught her foot and set her flat on her back. Momentarily he was entranced with the view. Then as she reached for the gun he kicked it out of her reach and came over and measured the contents of the bottle. "Cheating on me, hunh?"

McBride clapped hands. "The Marines to the rescue."

"I was a gob," Sweeney said. Neither paid the slightest attention to the cursing Sybil. Presently she stopped cursing and began to cry. After a while McBride got up, modestly wrapping the robe around him, and lifted her and put her on the chaise. "Tell papa, Beautiful." He poured her a good stiff drink.

She stared malevolently at Sweeney. "Where did you come from?"

"He's my bodyguard," McBride said.

Sweeney denied this. "I am not. I'm his valet." He took the bottle away from McBride. "And it's okay by me, babe, if you wanna be alone with him. Only not with my bottle." He retired to the bathroom.

McBride picked up Mrs. Nordstrom's bag, got a handkerchief out of it and dabbed at her eyes. The bag smelled of Passionette. He sat on the foot of the chaise. "A fine business, trying to shoot your best friend."

She began repairing the damage to her make-up. Her sea-green eyes were calculating. "What did you mean about Teal and Fenner?"

McBride wore an injured air. "I told you they were on board, didn't I? I even gave you the names they were using. God knows they've got as much interest in you as I have." He shrugged. "Maybe more."

She smoothed her lipstick with the tip of her little finger. "What happened after I passed out?"

"What usually happens after a gal passes out? If the guy with her is a gentleman he goes home." He leered. "I thought once about putting you to bed but I restrained myself."

Her hat had come off in the struggle with Sweeney. She patted her platinum hair into place. There were dark circles under her eyes. McBride thought these were the result of worry, not of the binge. He said angrily, "How come you just discovered you lost something? If it was that important why didn't you know it this morning, before we docked?"

She looked at him. "Because somebody was very clever; so clever that I thought it might be you. The original envelope was left, but there was nothing in it but blank paper."

He cursed. "What was supposed to be in it—a map of how to find your husband?"

Her eyes were inscrutable. "Yes," she said shortly. "Yes, that was it." She swung her long legs off the chaise. "Happen to know where Teal and Fenner are staying?"

"Not Fenner," he said. He got up and searched around for her little gun. Finding it, he tossed it into her lap. "Teal is at the Swanson House on Beretania Street. Name of George Craven."

The gun satisfied her. He had thought it would. She put it back in the bag, closed the bag with a snap. The sound was not loud but he was reminded of the jaws of a trap. In that moment he was almost sorry for George Teal.

She stood up. "I'm still thinking about you, Rex McBride. As soon as I figure out a way I'll let you know about this job I want you to do." She put her arms around him. "Sore at me, darling?"

"A little," he admitted. He freed himself, holding her wrists. "Dames with guns give me goose pimples."

"Kiss me?"

"Unh-unh, that gives me goose pimples too."

She laughed her brittle, tinkling little laugh. "That isn't what it gives me, darling." She moved to the hall door. "Dinner tonight?"

"Maybe."

She said a very unladylike word. "So you're being coy!"

"Just careful, Beautiful."

"I see that woman is still around."

McBride grinned. "Can I help it if I'm winsome?"

"You don't have to peddle it."

McBride almost hit her. Then he suddenly remembered that he was a patriot and didn't. It was a terrible handicap, being a patriot, though. He assumed the slightly ribald look of an amiable satyr. "I'm always open to offers, Beautiful. When you get ready to close the deal, let me know." He opened the door for her.

Closing it presently he saw that Sweeney had come out of the bath. Sweeney was very drunk. "You done noble, pal, noble." He hurled the empty bottle through the nearest window. The window was not open.

AND SUDDEN DEATH, XXII

It was shortly before nine o'clock and McBride was finishing a lonely dinner in the grill room of the Mauna Loa. There were several reasons for his dining in the grill. He wished, temporarily, to avoid both Miss Kay Ford and Mrs. Sybil Nordstrom, though for entirely different purposes. He had the uncomfortable feeling that there were eyes on him wherever he turned, eyes that were better not fixed on Miss Ford. It was small comfort to know that the white-haired Mr. Cord had promised help. Presumably this help consisted of an additional shadow on Mrs. Nordstrom. McBride had been unable to spot the man. Consequently he was relying on Sweeney to cover her for the short time necessary to eat. At home he would have had the hotel staff and a host of bell-hops, all eager to earn a more or less honest dollar by reporting on the lady's movements. Here the help was ninety per cent Oriental. There was no telling what effect an unguarded query would have.

For Mrs. Nordstrom herself, McBride was certain she would make no move so long as she was in his company. Perhaps the most important reason, though, for slighting the main dining room tonight was the matter of dress. A low-cut vest, either white or black, offers little concealment for a gun worn in the waistband of your trousers. McBride was carrying his gun steadily now. He was inconspicuous in blue flannels.

Around him were other diners, mostly men, either alone like himself or in twos and threes. The talk was all of the new and gigantic defense appropriations, of the relations of the South American countries with the United States, of the Panama Canal and, here in Hawaii, of the unwonted activities at the Pearl Harbor naval base. Nels Nordstrom and his two million ill-got dollars, in the perspective of recent events, was rapidly becoming of comparatively small importance, and herein lay the danger of losing him. The authorities were too busy with larger things to be concerned over the goings and comings of an ordinary absconder.

McBride, lost in gloom, was roused from his abstraction by the sudden and unheralded appearance of Lieutenant Stone of the Honolulu police. One moment he was quite alone; the next, Stone was there at his side, tall, self-possessed, polite as hell but vaguely menacing. "May I join you, Mr. McBride?"

"Sure." McBride pushed out a chair.

Stone ordered coffee, nothing else. Stirring it, he considered McBride. "We have been checking up on some very interesting radiograms. In the light of events aboard the *Honolulu Queen* I may say that these various messages have led us to an inevitable conclusion."

"Is that so?" McBride said. Inwardly he cursed Fourth Officer Rhys. He wished he hadn't hit the guy.

Stone lit a thin black cigar. "Take the one about the steward, an alleged suicide. A man named McGonigle, a man in Los Angeles, mind you, seemed to think it might be something else."

"Hell," McBride said disgustedly, "you ought to know these city editors. A murder is good for ten times as much space as a suicide. He was just hoping."

Stone nodded pleasantly. "You made inquiry about Baron Itsuki *before* his unfortunate end. You were informed that his address coincided with someone whose initials are S. N. I wonder if a lady by the name of Sybil Nordstrom could possibly fit those initials."

McBride didn't mind being a patriot, but he was damned if he was going to let an ordinary cop chisel into his game. He'd had trouble with cops before over the division of rewards and one thing and another. "What are you trying to get at?"

"That the Japanese spy business was nothing more than a red herring, Mr. McBride. A cleverly placed red herring, I'll grant you that. But if you ask me, the whole thing centers around a certain lady and her husband and the matter of some two million dollars."

McBride scowled. "Did I ask you?"

"I'm asking you," Stone pointed out.

"And I'm telling you to mind your own goddam business!"

Stone blew a smoke ring. "It is my business, Mr. McBride. Murder is always my business."

"If you mean Lord Fessenden——"

"Not Fessenden," Stone said. "A man named Teal, alias George Craven."

McBride's eyes were very bright. "Never heard of him."

"That is a lie, Mr. McBride."

"Prove it!"

Angry color darkened Stone's face. "All right, I will. This man Teal was also aboard the *Honolulu Queen*. He was intimately connected with Nordstrom in the looting of the Southern Counties Building & Loan of Hollywood. Released from Folsom six months ago he was on his way to contact Nordstrom, either for revenge or profit, and he interfered with you. You killed him."

McBride's ribald laughter echoed from the teak rafters. "It must be those cigars you smoke! What time was this guy killed?"

"At exactly seven o'clock. The shots were heard."

"And all this happened where?"

"In a room at the Swanson House."

McBride spread his hands. "I haven't been out of this hotel since noon. I can prove it."

Stone nodded. "I know that. We've already checked." He drew on his cigar. "I'm not accusing you of the actual deed. I am accusing you of engineering it. I must ask you to come downtown with me, Mr. McBride."

McBride looked at him. "Warrant?"

"Yes."

McBride pushed himself away from the table. "If I told you you were monkeying with a buzz saw, what would you say?"

"That it was another one of your clever little lies, Mr. McBride."

"I see." McBride stood up. "Use a phone, copper?"

"In my presence."

"Why not?" McBride said. He laid a bill on top of the check, turned to the phone booths in the passage between the grill and the main lobby. Presently he was in conversation with Mr. Cord at the Federal Building. "This guy," he complained, "a copper named Stone, is cramping my style."

"Let me talk to him," Cord said.

McBride passed the receiver to Stone. "Big shot," he explained casually. Stone, eyes never leaving McBride, listened to a barrage of words from the other end of the line. "All right," he said after a while. "Yes, I understand. Yes." He hung up. He was not happy. "You make friends rather quickly, Mr. McBride."

"I'm a patriot," McBride said smugly.

Stone lost his temper. "You are like hell! You're in this for money and you've killed God knows how many people." He let his shoulders droop. "Unfortunately, there's nothing I can do about it—now."

The way he stuck on that last word was a definite threat. He might be temporarily detoured. He wasn't stopped. McBride deliberately laid another mine. "I wouldn't feel too bad, copper. Why don't you look up a guy named Fenner? A very fat guy. He was traveling with Teal. Maybe he did it."

Stone looked at him. "You'd like to see Fenner dead too, wouldn't you? You'd use the whole police department; yes, even the Federal Government, by God, to further your own ends!"

"I'm a very nasty guy," McBride admitted. "Remember that if you get any more screwy ideas." He turned on his heel and crossed the lobby to the main dining room. Sybil Nordstrom was dining alone at a small table to the right of the orchestra. They were playing soft and sweet, a medley of Island melodies that tugged at your throat. Sweeney was furtively cutting his initials in the bole of a potted palm. McBride went up to his room.

As he unlocked the door he was conscious of wind in the room and he stood perfectly still for a moment. There were no lights. Vague shadows which might or might not be just the furniture loomed against the lesser blackness of the windows and a curtain flapped noisily in the breeze. It had been raining a little and the smell of warm rich loam was mixed with the tropic scent of flowers and the faint oily taint of fresh putty. The glaziers had repaired the window.

McBride presently decided that if anyone were waiting for him they would have struck before now. He made an excellent target, limned there against the brightness of the corridor. He reached in and snapped on the lights.

Except for the open window giving on the narrow second-story gallery the room appeared the same as when he had left it. Probably Sweeney, he thought. Or the wind. Shrugging, because he was a little irritated at his recent penchant for seeing bogies behind even the most common occurrence, he went over and closed the window and drew the blinds. The telephone rang.

It was Cord again. "See here, McBride, I'm not God, you know. My influence with the civil authorities can only be stretched so far. I don't want any more of this bushwhacking."

"What bushwhacking?"

Cord was exasperated. "You know what I'm talking about. Teal's murder. I don't know how you accomplished it but I'm satisfied that you did."

McBride raised his eyes and saw Saul Fenner in the bathroom door. The fat man had a gun as big as a cannon. McBride put the phone down very carefully. He did not cradle it, just laid it on the desk. "Hello," he said. He hoped Cord would know he was talking to someone else.

Fenner's eyes were on McBride's face. Except for their malevolence they were like raisins in a dish of pudding. The hand holding the gun was dimpled and creased, like a baby's hand, only ten times as large. "You shot George Teal," Fenner said. His voice was husky, practically a whisper, as though he might be suffering from some throat affliction.

McBride's hand inched toward the gun in his waistband. He wished now that he had used a shoulder clip. "Listen," he said angrily, "I'm getting a little tired of being accused of that. First the cops, now you!"

"The cops are smart too," Fenner whispered. He came a little way into the room, rocking slightly as very fat men often do. His feet, oddly enough, were quite small. Never once did he take his eyes off McBride's face. "Teal was my friend, McBride. You shot him."

McBride hooked a thumb in his belt. Fenner shook his head slightly. "If that's a gun you're feeling around for, don't."

"Why not?" McBride said. "You're not here for conversation."

"No, I'm not here for conversation. I'm here to even up for George Teal."

"Sure," McBride said recklessly. "You're here to even up for the kill of a dirty stinking murderer by the name of George Teal. Well, go ahead and get it over with, you fat bastard. Sure, I killed Teal. Not with my own hands, but I fixed it. Remember the little steward, Fenner? Remember little Simmons?"

"That was an accident," Fenner said. "I was as much responsible for that as Teal was. In fact it was I who broke his neck." He lifted the cannon. "Good-by, McBride."

There was a sudden terrific banging on the door. McBride thought that for just an instant Fenner's eyes moved, and he flipped the gun out of his pants. An invisible mailed fist came out of nowhere and slammed the gun back into his belly. Gagging, he folded in the middle and fell on his face. It seemed that iron fingers clamped his throat, shutting off his wind, and he flopped around there on the floor like a headless chicken. Vaguely he heard the sound of a shot. Then he and all else in the room became as nothing.

AND SUDDEN DEATH, XXIII

WHEN McBride could breathe again, or at least was conscious enough to know that he was breathing, and that it was an almost unbearable agony, he opened his eyes and stared straight into those of Lieutenant Stone. Stone was astride McBride's chest, giving him artificial respiration and cursing as eloquently as McBride himself could have done.

"Get—off—stomach!" McBride wheezed. He discovered that he was still on the floor. Beyond Stone there was quite a crowd, filling the doorway, spreading out into the hall. Inside the room itself were Sybil Nordstrom, Sweeney, Kay Ford and a young man McBride had never seen before. Wind from an open window flapped the curtains.

Stone got off McBride's stomach. Sweeney approached cautiously, tendering a nearly empty pint flask. McBride, on an elbow now, drained the flask with one gulp. He felt like a fool. Miss Ford came and knelt beside him. Her blue eyes were misty, as though she might have been crying. "Does it hurt so terribly, Rex?"

"You're damned right it hurts!" There was no use trying to be a stoic. That stuff was all right for heroes, but McBride could not consider himself a hero, especially with all these people catching him flat on his back. He put his hands on the floor and pushed himself to a sitting position. Violent nausea attacked him, because bending at the middle only aggravated the ache that was in him. Stone and Sweeney helped him stand up. His pants almost fell off. Embarrassed no end he caught his loosened belt and looked down at himself. Somebody had ripped his shirt and vest open, exposing his stomach as one vast angry bruise, shading away from a focal point that was an almost perfect impression of his own gun. He licked his lips. "Could you—could we close that damned door?"

Sweeney went over and closed it. The unidentified young man opened it again and went out. There was left in the room only McBride, Lieutenant Stone, Miss Ford, Sybil Nordstrom and Sweeney. From somewhere Sweeney produced a second flask. He did not offer this to McBride.

"Well?" Stone said. His eyes were angry.

McBride glared at him. "Fenner, copper. I told you!" He sucked air cautiously into his lungs. "He thought the same as you did—that I killed George Teal."

Stone nodded. "I gathered that." His eyes flicked the faces of those in the room. "Your side of the conversation was heard over the phone by a certain party. He caught me in the lobby downstairs and I came up."

"I heard you," McBride said nastily. "So did Fenner."

Stone flushed. "We'll get him, don't worry about that." He went over to the open window. There were a few bright drops of blood on the low sill. "You must have plugged him."

McBride stared. "If I did it was pure reflex action. His slug hit my gun and after that I didn't know a damned thing." He frowned on Miss Ford. "What are you doing here?"

"I live next door, remember?"

Sybil Nordstrom explained her own presence with a malicious little smile for Kay Ford. "The shots, you know. Everybody heard them. Naturally, darling, I knew that wherever there was shooting I would find you. You're so impulsive."

Sweeney waved the flask. The gesture said that he was a detective assigned to tail a lady, and that, come flood or famine, he would not fail the trust. He brazenly took another drink, wiping his lips daintily afterward on the back of his hand.

McBride put both hands on his stomach, removed them immediately. He wondered if he would have to go on standing up the rest of his life. Miss Ford quietly let herself out of the room. Her eyes bothered McBride. He looked at Stone. "Well, you won't find the guy around here."

"There are others on the force beside me," Stone said. "Quite a lot of them, McBride. You'd do well to remember that."

Their eyes met briefly. They were armed belligerents, just resting a moment, getting their wind for an inevitable and decisive conflict. Presently Stone swung toward the door. "A doctor could tape you up so you'd be almost as good as new, McBride. Shall I send one up?"

"It's a thought," McBride admitted. "Thanks."

Stone went out. Already the crowd in the hall had been dispersed. Except for McBride's stomach and the open gallery window and the few bright drops of blood on the sill the whole thing might never have been. Someone had even replaced the phone in its cradle.

Sybil Nordstrom moved lazily over to the window. "Was it really Fenner, McBride?"

"What do you think?"

"You told me you would take care of both of them, remember? I didn't know you meant to make it a public affair."

McBride snatched the bottle out of Sweeney's fist. "Quit it, you lush!" He drank thirstily, offered the remainder to Mrs. Nordstrom. She shook her head, then changed her mind and had herself a slug. She set the bottle on the desk, touched her lips with a Passionette-scented handkerchief. "So where does this leave us, darling?"

"Hell's fire," he said angrily, "how did I know Fenner was in love with Teal? And anyway, what difference does it make? That damn Rhys supplied the local cops with enough additional information so that when Teal was found they naturally tried to pin it on me. So I told 'em it was Fenner. You and I are still in the clear."

Her sea-green eyes narrowed a little. "Are we, darling?" She looked at Sweeney, dismissed him as though he were a wooden Indian. "Just who is this 'certain party' your friend Lieutenant Stone mentioned?"

McBride inwardly cursed Stone. Not that the slip was necessarily Stone's fault. He had no means of knowing that Mrs. Nordstrom was the key to the whole business. McBride shrugged. "Just a guy."

She persisted. "The young man who was up here, perhaps? The one who so conveniently disappeared afterward?"

That was bad too. McBride had no doubt that the young man in question was one of Mr. Cord's young men, but he couldn't very well tell Sybil Nordstrom that. Still, shaped properly, an explanation which included the young man could be made fairly convincing. "All right," he said sulkily, "I hired the guy from a private agency. You're not trusting me with much, Beautiful. I'm not trusting you either."

She laughed at that. "Nothing like honesty, is there, darling?"

"I wouldn't know, babe," McBride grinned. "I'm a private dick, myself."

There was a knock on the door. Opening it, Sweeney admitted the house physician. He was a youngish man, very dapper. "A Lieutenant Stone asked me to come up."

"Sure," McBride said. "Sure, come on in." He offered the doctor a drink, but it was refused. Sweeney was vastly relieved. "You'd think that stuff grew on trees around here!"

Sybil Nordstrom yawned daintily. "Well, I'll toddle along. See you later, darling?"

"Sure," McBride said. "I'll be up in a little while." He knocked Sweeney's hand away from the bottle. "See Mrs. Nordstrom to her room, lush."

"Lush, yourself!"

"Really," Mrs. Nordstrom protested, "I don't need——"

"Of course not," McBride agreed. "Just the same," he added stubbornly, "Sweeney's got to learn to be a gentleman. How can he learn if he doesn't practice?" He bared his torso for the doctor. Mrs. Nordstrom went out, Sweeney stalking her with a lecherous leer.

"This looks bad," the doctor commented. He kept poking at McBride's belly and flanks. "We should have X-rays."

McBride sucked in his breath. "Some other time, pal. If you think there's any loose parts floating around in there just strap 'em up where you think they ought to be. I'll pose for the art studies later."

The doctor was intrigued with McBride's scars. "War?"

"In a way," McBride said. He'd been exactly eleven years old at the time of the last war. He'd made a lot of money selling papers. The doctor got out bandage and adhesive. He was unnecessarily rough, McBride thought. The sweat stood out like dew on the McBride brow by the time the job was finished. He went over and picked up the bottle and drained it. "Looks like somebody else will have to tie my shoes for a while."

"You've got a valet, haven't you?"

McBride made a bitter mouth. "That guy!" Getting out a fresh shirt he was surprised to find that he didn't feel so bad at that. He didn't know whether this was due to Sweeney's rye or the doctor's ministrations. Once, on a trouble-shooting job for the gas company, he had ridden a motorcycle and worn a bucking belt. This makeshift corset was kind of like that. He was okay as long as he didn't bend too sharply in the middle. He paused on his way to the bathroom. "Thanks, Doc. Have it put on my bill, will you?"

The doctor said that he would do this. He snapped his bag closed and went out. Presently, arrayed anew and with a very military carriage indeed, McBride slipped his gun into his shoulder clip and was just turning toward the door when Sweeney burst in.

Sweeney was outraged. "She gimme the slip! The blonde wench tricked me!"

McBride's voice was heavy with sarcasm. "So you came here looking for her?"

Sweeney purpled. "You said I should be a gentleman, didn't you? And no gent follows a lady into the bathroom, do they?"

McBride prayed loudly for strength. "Tell me exactly what happened, lug!"

Sweeney took a long breath. "Well, she ast me in, and then we had a couple drinks and this and that. Then she says, very embarrassed like, would I excuse her a minute, and goes into the bath." He spread his hands. "Well, so naturally I think she's gotta go, and besides I never seen a bathroom window yet that anything bigger'n a cat could get through." He avoided McBride's eyes. "Only I forgot there was another door. Seems she just went through it into the next room."

From far down the drive came the sound of a shot. Two more followed it in quick succession. McBride swung through the open window to the narrow gallery. A cocoanut palm slanted up from the darkness below, obviously the means used by Fenner to gain access to the room. McBride thought that if Fenner could climb it, he, McBride, could certainly slide down. He proved his theory at the expense of scratched hands and a torn sleeve. Sweeney used the more direct method of dropping unaided from the gallery rail. They landed ankle-deep in a soggy flower bed, extricated themselves and pounded down the winding gravel drive.

Lights were winking on in some of the bungalows of the annex but as yet no one was outside. Rounding the first turn McBride saw ahead of him the glowing twin tail lamps of a stationary car. Apparently there was some sort of obstruction before it. Beyond that, swift shadows moved; a car's motor roared; then there was silence, unbroken save for McBride's and Sweeney's running feet.

Coming to the car they found it blocked by a second car, crosswise of the driveway. On either hand was the tall border of royal palms, impregnable to anything less than a tank. Beyond the right-hand row of trees stretched tropical jungle, left as God made it, dark and forbidding. The whole was an ideal spot for an ambush. From up the drive, toward the hotel, came shouts of men and the shriller tones of women.

Cursing, McBride ran around the blocked car. He almost fell over a man on his hands and knees. The guy was a veritable giant, even in that position. He had a great shaggy black beard and he kept shaking his head from side to side, like a groggy but still defiant bull. Blood streamed down over his face from a deep gash in the top of his head. He was in oil-stained dungarees. McBride hauled him back on his haunches, was almost knocked flat by one of the big man's flailing arms. Sweeney fell on top of the giant. McBride was making sibilant little sounds through his teeth. "Let him up, lug."

Sweeney got up. The big man just sat there for a moment, breathing gustily. Presently he began to curse fluently in what sounded like Rusian.

McBride took out his gun. "So you're the Czar of Russia now!"

"Sure." The giant pounded his chest. "Boronoff, me!"

"You are like hell," McBride said. "You've put on a lot of weight and bought yourself a bottle of dye, but you're still Nels Nordstrom to me. I'm very glad to meet you, pal. I've been looking all over for you."

What happened after that was always a black spot

in McBride's memory. He had a gun. Sweeney had a gun. There were two of them against one. And Nels Nordstrom got up and held out his two hands, wrists close together as if for the manacles. "All right," he said, "you've got me." McBride and Sweeney stepped in. They stepped right into two of the most devastating back-hands that either had ever experienced. When they finally stopped rolling Nels Nordstrom was gone. He was gone so completely that there was not even a rustle from the tangled undergrowth beyond the palms.

Lieutenant Stone and the young man from Mr. Cord's office were in the vanguard of the hotel contingent. McBride was scrabbling around in the gravel, trying to find his gun. His jaws were clamped so tight they hurt.

"What goes on?" Stone demanded. "What are you looking for?"

"My hat," McBride said. "You see it anywhere, Sweeney?"

"Damn you, McBride," Stone yelled, "you can't do this to me. I won't have it!"

McBride was in no mood to take anything from anybody. He had just had two million dollars in his hands and let it slip through his fingers. He stabbed a hard forefinger at Stone's chest. "Listen, copper, we heard a couple of shots. We ran down here. The two cars were just like you see them and a bunch of guys got away in a third. You take it from there."

Stone teetered on his heels. "So you and your man Friday just fell down!"

"The name is Sweeney," Sweeney said sullenly.

The unidentified young man had again disappeared. He was the most retiring young man McBride had ever seen. Stone went around and peered at the registration of both cars. "U-Drives!" he muttered. "Well, maybe we can get something from them at that." He came back to face McBride. "What did these men look like?"

McBride found that he could answer this one quite truthfully. "I don't know, Lieutenant. They were no more than shadows."

"I'll bet!" Stone sneered.

"All right," McBride yelled, "they were a company of Marines from the barracks, then!" He swung up the drive, not caring what happened to Stone, Sweeney or anybody else.

In his room he regarded sourly the wreckage of what had once been a beautiful suit of blue flannels. He started to change, decided he wouldn't, decided he would. He thought angrily of Mr. Cord and Mr. Cord's young men. He wondered what had happened to Sybil Nordstrom; to her husband Nels in his outlandish Russian getup; to Fenner and Chalice O'Connor and all the rest of them. He wished he had never become a patriot.

After a while, once more presentable in a suit of gray-green gabardine, he went to the phone and ordered a bottle and some ice sent up. Sweeney came in on the heels of the Filipino who delivered them. He licked his lips. "For me?"

"For why?" McBride demanded. "What did you ever do for your country?"

"I was a gob, wasn't I?"

McBride made a very undignified sound with his lips. "I notice you got out before the war started." He tipped the boy, saw him out the door.

"So that was the broad's old man," Sweeney observed. His eyes kindled. "Jesus, what he could do to Joe Louis!"

"The hell with Louis," McBride grunted. "Look what he did to us. A fine pair of palookas we are!"

"Oh, I don't know," Sweeney said complacently. "I can tell you a lot about that guy. He fools around with boats."

McBride was skeptical. "Oh, yeah?"

"Well, he does," Sweeney insisted. "Motorboats. Them dungarees of his smelled of 'em, and don't tell me no different. I was in the Navy."

McBride poured some of the liquor into a tumbler. "Bragging again, hunh?" He offered the glass to Sweeney who accepted it as his just due.

The telephone rang. It was Mr. Cord calling. "What's this I hear, McBride?"

McBride's eyes smoldered with resentment. "Oh, so your Number One boy reported, did he? I understood you were going to give me some help on this job."

Cord sounded apologetic. "It was just one of those things, I guess. She got away clean?"

"And not only her," McBride said. "I'm out a couple of million bucks too." He thought a minute. "Unless you can find me a boat that this guy belongs to. Calls himself Boronoff and looks like the ex-Czar of all the Russias, only he's got blue eyes. My—uh—helper says he plays around with motorboats."

"You tell Stone that?"

McBride swore. "I wouldn't tell that guy anything. I'd as soon have Nordstrom get away as have that mug make the pinch. Either way I'd lose."

Cord became very confidential. "And what of the other?"

"We've got one more chance. If you don't muff it, that is. They'll be around."

"You think these men who got away were Japanese?"

"I don't think they were Eskimos," McBride said. He hung up and repaired to the bed. Sweeney carefully and very fairly divided the liquor into two equal parts, using one of the empty pint flasks to measure by. He then retired to the chaise longue.

"So we're expecting company, hunh?"

"Maybe," McBride said. He switched off the lights.

AND SUDDEN DEATH, XXIV

It was not late. It merely seemed so, because so much had happened in a comparatively short time. Lying there in the dark, listening to the small, once more normal, sounds of a great hotel, listening to Sweeney's even breathing become a gentle snore, McBride took account of himself and found the result far from good.

Cord is right, he thought. I'm just a stumble-bum. Curiously it did not occur to him actually to blame Cord for the way things had turned out. He had pretended to, but it was nothing more than a sop to his own vanity. It was his fault; his and Sweeney's. They had actually had Nordstrom in their hands. He dismissed the giant Nordstrom temporarily and took up the matter of Sybil.

Obviously she was caught in a net of espionage and intrigue that was far and away more perilous than the game of hide-and-seek which involved her husband. How she had got into the thing originally McBride could not even guess. Money, perhaps, had been the initial motivation; money offered for the performance of a seemingly unimportant act. Later, like the piling up of lies, one upon the other, the little jobs became greater ones and she was enmeshed beyond her power to withdraw.

Casting back, McBride was able to see things now that had not been apparent before. Sybil Nordstrom was afraid, deathly afraid, of the man or men who controlled her actions. The way she had said: "Itsuki was no friend of mine." Her repeated attempts to commit McBride in the matter of hiring himself out as a killer. She wanted to escape and couldn't. This indicated a leverage of some sort, a threat of exposure that was even more to be feared than the organization of which she was a part. In other words, a killing would not free her. She must possess herself of the instrument, the proof of her own complicity. Possibly she had been promised this in return for carrying that certain envelope through the port officials. And then came the inevitable discovery that the envelope contained nothing but blank paper.

No wonder she had been desperate; so desperate indeed that she had accused McBride directly, knowing full well that if he had made the substitution he must know what she was. In her highly emotional state it had been easy enough to convince her of either Teal's guilt, or Fenner's. And she had relayed the information to those above her. McBride was not sorry for Teal's killing. The man was a murderer. He had paid with his own life. Fenner's own admission was proof, if McBride had needed further proof, that both men were responsible for the murder of little Simmons.

McBride turned over on his side and picked up the bottle. He put it down again without drinking. His mind was functioning at high enough speed without the artificial stimulus of liquor. In the maelstrom he himself had created, it had seemed logical that Nels

Nordstrom would appear; that centrifugal force, if nothing else, would draw the man into the vortex. Well, it had. Sybil Nordstrom had taken the bit in her teeth and run for it. Her husband had hidden out for over three years; with his help she too could escape the consequences of her own acts. She would be hunted; she would be unable to spend the money as she would have liked to; but at least she would be safe.

So much for Sybil's own reactions. And here, McBride thought, was a strange contradiction; a train of thought of which only an unnerved woman could be capable. The very thing she feared most she had discounted. She had actually believed it possible that they would leave her unguarded. And she had been caught.

McBride, forgetting his bruised mid-section, sat erect. He almost passed out as sharply sickening pain stabbed at his vitals. He lay down again, breathing evenly till the nausea had left him. Then by a series of corkscrew convolutions he attained his feet and picked up the phone and called Cord. "You all set?"

"There are half-a-dozen men out there."

"I'm going to leave the room for a little while. Sweeney will be here."

"That's not so good," Cord objected. "If you're seen leaving the room——"

"I won't be," McBride promised. "Not by anybody except our own people." He took a breath. "Maybe not even them if I'm as good as I think I am. I just got a hunch."

"Well——"

"Thanks," McBride said. He hung up. Presently he went very quietly to the door and opened it the barest crack. Down at the end of the corridor the drapes over a window embrasure moved ever so slightly. He closed the door again and went to the French windows opening on the gallery. So far as he could tell there was no one out there. Cord's men would be in the halls and down in the gardens, because the object was to trap the expected intruders after they had gained admission, not to scare them away before. A certain amount of leeway was thus necessary. If the cordon were closed too tightly no one would try to get through.

He went back and shook Sweeney gently. "I'm shoving off for a while, sailor. Watch it. And lay off the liquor, you hear me?"

"Okay," Sweeney said. "You know me, tutz."

"That's the trouble," McBride complained. He went back to the windows and stood there for a moment, looking out. Far away through the tall trees the lights of a beach car winked briefly. Then it was blacker than seven hundred dollars again. The air smelled of rain. McBride moved silently out to the gallery, crouching so that the rail partially obscured him. This crouching business was not so good; it was, in fact, painful as hell and he resolved to get it over with as soon as possible. There were no lights in Miss Ford's room. Passing it he wondered if she were asleep. Probably not, he thought. She's probably down in some bar having herself a time while I'm being a patriot. A fine business!

He went on, more swiftly now that he was away from the immediate vicinity of his own room. A couple of windows that were lighted offered a momentary hazard, but nobody screamed or offered to shoot him. Presently he came to a fire exit, another pair of French windows. The drawn drapes inside glowed faintly ruby. He put a steady, even pressure against the joint of the two sections. The catch snapped. He went in then, and stood for a little while, breathing easily, screened by the heavy curtains. A man and a woman passed him, so close he could have reached out and touched them. Down the corridor the elevator gates opened, closed.

After a time he shed his concealment and went swiftly but not furtively up the rear stairs to the third floor. Up here there was even less movement than there had been on the floor below. He paused just outside Sybil Nordstrom's room and lit a cigarette. There was no sound from within. It was a little strange, he thought, that in all this time no one had noted Sybil's absence. Certainly Stone knew about her; Saul Fenner too, and the girl, Chalice O'Conner. None of these, of course, knew of the Japanese espionage angle, though Stone may have guessed.

McBride wondered if the door had been locked. He decided not to try it except as a last resort. Remembering Sweeney's explanation of the way she had lost him, hoping that the room next door was still untenanted, McBride moved down to it and tested the knob. It turned under his hand and he went in as silently as a shadow. No one rose out of the darkness to challenge him. There was the indefinable smell of a room without occupants. After a time, his eyes now accustomed to the faint light from the windows, he crossed the room and entered the connecting bath, closing the door after him. The opposite door was wide open. He wondered a little at this; wondered if he were too early or too late. Beyond the door someone drew a deep breath, let it out quickly. McBride flipped his cigarette through the opening, watched it burst into a shower of sparks against the far wall. Then he was inside and behind the giant with the knife. "Nordstrom!"

The man stood perfectly still. He had been sitting in a chair, facing the hall door. He was still facing the door but the cigarette had brought him to his feet. "I don't want to have to shoot you," McBride said. "Drop the knife."

The bright sliver of steel fell to the carpet. Only then did McBride move in, and he moved as swiftly, as daintily as a toe dancer. His gun lifted, chopped down, once, twice. It was as simple as that. Nordstrom sank to the floor without even a groan. McBride let out his breath with a tremendous whooshing sound. "Christ!" He discovered that he was shaking from head to foot. There was the smell of burning wool where the cigarette gnawed at the carpet. McBride went over and stepped on it.

Presently he snapped on the lights and ripped a sheet off the bed and went about the business of securing a potential two million dollars. As he finished the last knot he saw Nordstrom's eyelids flutter. "That was kind of a dirty trick, pal, only you fooled me last time. Sorry."

Nordstrom's eyes opened all the way. "Not your fault. It was she who tricked me."

McBride sighed. He felt a little like David must have when he slew Goliath. "Like a drink, pal?"

"Please."

McBride got up and went to the bath and filled a glass. He held the big man's head up till the last drop was gone. He then put a pillow under the head, lit a cigarette and stuck it between bearded lips. Nordstrom's eyes thanked him.

McBride stared at nothing in particular. "She didn't trick you, Nels. She was trying to escape something bigger than she was, bigger than any of us, for that matter, and it caught up with her, that's all."

Nordstrom rolled his head a little to avoid the drifting smoke. "I wish I could believe that."

McBride nodded. "I know what you thought. I'd probably have thought the same thing in your place. That's how I got here. I just wondered what I would do if I were you. The answer was I'd cut her heart out. So I came up."

Nordstrom eyed him curiously. "What's your angle?"

"I'm after the dough," McBride said. "I'm working for people who have a legal right to it. There have been others with not so good a claim: Fenner, Teal, a girl named Chalice O'Connor whose old man is still in the can because of you." He lit two more cirgarettes, one for himself this time. They smoked quietly for a moment. "In a way," McBride said, "I've done you a favor. You'd either have killed or been killed in the end. This way, if you're ready to deal, you can take a rap of two-to-ten and be through with it."

"Prop me up?" Nordstrom said.

"Sure." McBride hauled the big man to a sitting position and pushed an ottoman behind his back. Nordstrom had got himself cleaned up somewhere. He was no longer wearing the oily dungarees. The dyed hair on top of his head was still matted with blood, though, from a shallow bullet crease. McBride's gun had opened the wound again.

"Tell me," Nordstrom said, "about my wife."

McBride's face was wooden. "You might be happier if you didn't know, pal. Why not forget it?"

"No."

"All right," McBride said harshly, "you're asking for it and I'll give it to you. She's been running with a bunch of Japanese spies and she was in a spot. Her only out was to trick them and go into hiding with you. She was on her way when they caught up with her."

Nordstrom sucked in his breath. "And I thought—"

McBride couldn't look at him for a minute. "I know. It looked like she'd deliberately led you into a police trap. You wake up and there are two guys standing over you, and she is gone." He went on rather hurriedly. "Tell you what I'll do. Lay the dough on the line for me and I'll try to get her as short a rap as possible. You'll both come out of it together."

"But you say she's in a spot!"

"She is, pal, and don't think I'm kidding you. All I can guarantee is a try."

Nordstrom spat out his cigarette. "It's a deal."

McBride touched his shoulder. "It's a deal, pal." He went to the phone. Behind him Nordstrom cursed suddenly. McBride whirled. Chalice O'Connor was standing in the hall door. The same little gun she had had on the *Honolulu Queen* was in her small fist now. "Don't move, Mr. McBride."

He glared at her. "I told you to stay out, you little fool. I meant it."

She shook her head. "For a time I almost believed you. But now I know better. You killed Teal. Fenner told me."

"Fenner's a goddam liar!"

"Am I?" Saul Fenner said. He blocked the bathroom door. His fat gun-hand hung loosely at his side. "I see my first slug didn't take, shamus. Let's try it again."

McBride was unhampered by an overlapping vest this time. His gun was not wedged against his belly.

Perhaps that is what fooled Fenner. Perhaps McBride was just the swifter of the two. He shot the fat man square in the mouth. And then, almost in the same motion, he hurled the gun at the girl and followed it with his body. He caught her as she swayed toward him, eyes closed, trying with all her might to squeeze the trigger of her little gun. She wasn't hit; she was only a very, very sick little girl.

McBride slapped her sharply. "Get out, keed. Get out now, before the cops get here. Nordstrom is coming clean. Get out and forget it." He pushed her through the door, closed and locked it, went back to the phone with not even a glance at the body of Saul Fenner.

Nordstrom began to laugh suddenly, hugely. "By God, McBride, you know something? I'm glad I dropped that knife!"

McBride replaced the phone. "Cops," he said sourly. "A dick named Stone. Don't let him kid anybody it was him that took you. He'll try it, the bastard."

There was a tremendous pounding on the door. McBride opened it to stare slack-jawed, not at Lieutenant Stone, but at Sweeney. "Well, for Christ's sake, what are you doing here?"

"The shots!" Sweeney gasped. "Heard the shots!" His breath caught in his throat, choking him. "Christ, McBride, they've got her!"

"Got who?"

"Her," Sweeney said thickly. "The lady."

AND SUDDEN DEATH, XXV

THEY were in McBride's room, just the four of them: McBride himself, Sweeney, Lieutenant Stone and the white-haired, brown-skinned Mr. Cord. Perhaps half an hour had elapsed; a half hour crammed with recriminations, hurled accusations and bitter retorts. Nels Nordstrom was safely in jail; Saul Fenner in the morgue. Of Chalice O'Connor there had been no further sign. Presumably she had at last taken McBride's advice.

McBride moved around the room with short, nervous strides, unable to be still a moment, feeling the anger well and seethe inside him till it was a terrible thing; anger at himself, at Cord, even at Kay Ford. Oddly too, for one who claimed to be as unsusceptible as McBride, there was a sickish feeling in the pit of his stomach that was not wholly due to the terrific beating caused by Saul Fenner's slug in that first encounter.

They were all on edge, with the possible exception of Cord. His smooth brown face mirrored no emotion whatever; his calm eyes watched McBride much as a scientist regards an interesting though relatively unimportant experiment.

Lieutenant Stone was angry and took no trouble to hide it. His suave mask had long since slipped. He watched Sweeney, who had been drinking steadily with no visible effect. "Tell me again exactly what was said."

Sweeney scowled at him. "I've told you a dozen times already. The phone rang and a guy asked for McBride."

"The voice was Japanese?"

"Christ," McBride snapped, "why go all over that again? Of course the voice was Japanese! The rest of it's all washed up."

"I'm not so sure," Stone said.

Sweeney flung the bottle from him. "Listen, flat-foot, if the boss says it's so, it's so!" He glowered at Cord, refusing to acknowledge Stone's right to question him further. "So I said McBride was out, and then I heard her say: 'Sweeney, tell him not to——' " Sweeney stared uncomfortably at McBride's wooden face. "Somebody smacked her in the mouth before she could finish. I heard it. Then the Jap's voice again: 'Tell Mr. McBride we will call him later.' "

Stone persisted. "You're sure it was Miss Ford?"

"I don't think it was no hula dancer."

McBride went on with his restless prowling. They were waiting now for the second phone call, hoping to trace it as it came in. Inquiry at the switchboard downstairs had accomplished nothing in the way of tracing the first. The girl had tried; they had all watched her trying, but too much time had elapsed before they had started checking. There were two of Cord's men on the board now.

Lieutenant Stone got up and went to the windows. The promised rain was falling, gently, almost without sound. The air was heavy with the fragrance of night-blooming jasmine. Stone said, "What do you suppose brought the man Fenner up to Mrs. Nordstrom's room?"

"How do I know?" McBride yelled. "Maybe he saw the lights from outside. Maybe he saw Nordstrom go up."

"It seems to me——"

McBride controlled himself with an effort. "You said that. It seems to you I should have tapped him on the wrist." He took a breath. "Look, copper, after what happened to me the first time I wasn't exactly calling my shots."

"I think maybe you were," Stone said nastily. "You accused Fenner of Teal's murder. He can't very well deny it now, can he?"

McBride just looked at him for a moment. "Sore because I beat you to Nordstrom?"

"Certainly not."

"You wouldn't be interested in a cut of the gravy?"

"No."

"Then you're not a copper. I never saw one yet that——" He broke off as the phone rang. Stone reached for it and McBride knocked his hand aside. "Mine, copper." His eyes were suddenly haggard. "Yes?"

There was a polite sucking of breath at the other end. "McBride gentoman, prease?"

"Talking."

"Young lady say she like seeing you some more. Say you like seeing her, you bring papers you take from ozzer lady."

McBride wet his lips. "I haven't got them."

"Can get, no?"

"No."

Again that polite hiss. "So sorry. So sorry for young lady."

McBride's hands were shaking. As through a haze he saw Cord at the door, poised, ready for word from below. Stone chewed savagely at his nails. Sweeney was working the action of McBride's automatic. McBride's voice was scarcely recognizable as he said, "All right, what do I do with them?"

"You come King Street fish markets." The line suddenly went dead. McBride jiggled the breaker. "Hey!" A new voice broke in: "You can hang up now, Mr. McBride. It's a public phone on Kapiolani Boulevard. We may catch our man in the vicinity."

McBride banged the phone down. Cord was talking to a man in the hall. He turned presently and looked at Lieutenant Stone. "The fish markets. Lots of territory down there."

Stone glanced at his strap watch. "Two o'clock. The markets will be opening up too. Hell of a note."

The phone rang. Cord went to it. Everybody in the room could hear the man's voice on the wire. "No dice, sir. The man was a Japanese. That's all we've been able to learn."

Cord replaced the instrument slowly. McBride's eyes were feverish. "There's no use asking you for that stuff back again, is there?"

"You know better than that, McBride."

"Sure." He laughed harshly. "Sure, I know better than that. What's a life more or less to the government?"

Cord's mouth made a thin straight line. "It wouldn't do any good anyway, McBride. You ought to know that. Our only hope is to cover you as best we can and pick up somebody we can sweat."

"You've been covering me all night!"

"Was that our fault?" Cord asked patiently. "You yourself expected them to strike at you. As a matter of fact, the girl never entered into it."

McBride went over and took the automatic away from Sweeney. "You guys can play games, be diplomats or anything you want to. I'll take a couple of rods for mine." He switched the two guns, leaving one in the shoulder clip. The other, the smaller one, he shoved in his belt at the small of his back. Even with his coat buttoned there was no bulge.

"We'll tail you, of course," Stone said.

McBride looked at him. "I'll put a slug in the first man that tries it. I've had a shot at being a patriot. Now I'm just a guy with a gun."

Cord blocked the door. He was still wearing the wrinkled pongee suit. He looked like nothing so much as a congressman from the South who had gotten elected because he was a Man of the Peepul. "I understand your attitude, McBride. I'm sorry that things have turned out the way they have. But our object in this business is to effect the capture of the ringleaders. You are not going to toss our best chance out the window."

McBride chewed at a knuckle. "Like that, hunh?"

"Like that," Cord said. He considered McBride's flushed face. "The district you are going into is a big one, teeming with Japanese. What do you think one man can do?"

"All right," McBride said savagely, "put a tail on me and what happens? They don't make contact!"

"Naturally I've thought of that," Cord said quietly. "You won't be tailed from here. But between the time you leave and the time you arrive there will be a number of our men already in the district. They won't interfere with you."

Stone said, "I think that's a mistake."

Cord's eyes hardened a little. "I don't give a damn what you think, Lieutenant." He moved his bulk from the doorway. "Good hunting, McBride."

McBride paused at the door. "Where the hell is this bunch of fish markets?"

"On North King, near River," Cord said. "You must have passed close to it as you left the boat." He looked at his watch again. "My car is at the main entrance. A Buick phaeton. Use that."

McBride went out. Crossing the almost deserted lobby downstairs he was again conscious of eyes. Aside from the night clerk and two men who were drunk and arguing politics he was the only white man. The girl at the switchboard, the bell-hops, even the elevator boys were Japanese or Filipinos. They all seemed to be watching him with more than ordinary interest. Shrugging off the feeling he went out to the lanai and descended to the drive. There were two other cars beside Cord's. One bore the official insignia of the police department. There was a cop behind the wheel.

McBride opened the door of the Buick and climbed in. Presently he was rolling down the drive, slowly at first, because he wanted to see if the police car would follow. It didn't. Passing the row of bungalows, rounding into the second turn of the twisting drive, a pair of headlights smacked him in the eyes. They were coming quite fast and instinctively he slowed, pulling far over to the right. Something landed on the right-hand running board, softly, with scarcely a jar. Turning he saw a grinning Japanese face, but even as he reached for his gun there was another thud behind him, this time on the lefthand running board. The headlights slid on past. Something banged McBride's skull solidly. He slumped over on the wheel. The last he remembered was the blaring of the horn.

When consciousness finally claimed him again it seemed that the horn was still ringing in his ears, though such reason as he had told him that this could not be. He was no longer in a car. A soft glow bathed his eyelids gratefully and, surprisingly, his head scarcely ached at all. Some liquid dripped between his open lips, faintly bitter but not unpleasant. He swallowed.

"Ni-ice," said a tinkling little voice.

McBride opened his eyes. He thought at first that he must be in the Japanese equivalent of Heaven. The girl with the spoon was a delicate flower; an houri; a petite and gracious Oriental angel. Her flowing kimono sleeves fell away from slender but beautifully rounded arms. Her eyes laughed at him. There was a tall, finely wrought comb in her hair. "Christ, you're beautiful!" McBride said. He would have said it on his deathbed. It occurred to him, remembering, that maybe he was on his deathbed. He discovered that he was not on a bed at all, but on a floor mat. His hands and feet were bound.

"Hah!" he said. "A fine business!"

"Sank you," she tinkled. She lifted the bottle in her left hand. "You like more?"

"What is it?" He tried to read the label on the bottle, gave it up as he saw that it was Japanese. She refused to commit herself on the contents of the bottle but she allowed him two more spoonfuls. He began to glow pleasantly. "Remind me to take some of that along, will you, Beautiful?" He didn't think he was going any place. Whoever had knocked him over had found both guns. He knew this because he was lying on his back and there was no lump except for the one made by his bound fists.

Beautiful got up and padded softly away. Not being able to look at her any more, McBride examined his surroundings. The room reminded him of the Japanese tea houses at World's Fairs. There were several mats such as the one he was on; a great teak and gold screen; a few slender taborets. The walls were sliding panels of translucent gray rice paper. McBride thought it would be a cinch to kick a hole through one of these. Sandalwood incense smoldered in a flat brass bowl.

One of the panels slid open and a man stepped through. The man was Baron Ito Itsuki. McBride stared at him without surprise. "You son of a bitch!"

Itsuki smiled. It was not his regulation smile, because he had shaved off his mustache. Also his skin was darker, as though it might have been tinted. "You are not startled, my friend?"

McBride spat. "I always understood the nobility, even the Japanese nobility, were honorable men. Thank Christ I was born in a gutter."

From beyond one of the walls Miss Ford said, "Rex!"

McBride wondered if they'd broken any of her fingers yet, like the maid's back in Los Angeles. He wondered if anybody would hear her if she screamed.

Itsuki came over and kicked him in the ribs. It hurt like hell. "You have caused me no end of trouble, my friend. I do not find those certain documents upon your person."

"I'm not crazy," McBride said. "Turn us loose and maybe I'll remember what I did with them."

Itsuki kicked him again. "You will remember, my friend. There are ways of stimulating the most fickle of memories." He was very careful to keep away from McBride's feet. McBride thought once about rolling over and biting a chunk out of an ankle, but it hardly seemed worth while. Itsuki moved lightly around the room. "Tell me, when did you first guess that I was not in a watery grave?"

"After you conked Miss Ford in Sybil Nordstrom's cabin. Mrs. Nordstrom was so sure that the lady had been inside. She could not have known this unless someone told her; obviously the assailant himself. It wasn't Fenner, nor was it Teal. Mrs. Nordstrom didn't even know they were aboard until I mentioned it. Then there were the marks of fingers on her throat. In the light of the later attack these could have been put there after your alleged death, not before. So I concluded you were no gentleman and had gone up under the bridge wing instead of down over the side. You are quite an athlete."

"But you did not notify the ship's officers?"

"That was my mistake," McBride said. "I figured I was pulling your teeth when I copped the stuff. Besides, I needed Mrs. Nordstrom on the loose. Jailed as a spy she couldn't lead me to her old man."

"Then too, perhaps, you had hopes of realizing a little something from the sale of the documents?"

McBride thought bitterly that even by a Japanese spy he was considered a crook. "I had hopes you might look me up," he admitted. This, incidentally, was truth in all its purity. He had salved his conscience in the matter of delay by promising himself a postponed but no less dire vengeance when the baron should try to recover the stuff. Going to Cord; in other words, becoming a patriot, had been quite a sacrifice.

Itsuki sighed. "It is pleasant to get these little matters straightened out before we begin on the larger ones." He rubbed his hands lightly together. "For myself, I hid in a lifeboat. Such food as I had was furnished me by our mutual and charming friend. It was very uncomfortable."

McBride sucked in his breath politely. "So sorry."

Itsuki laughed delightedly. "You are so clever, my friend. You would have appreciated the manner in which I left the ship." He washed his hands. "I simply became a native diver among the so many other native divers. Is that not funny?"

"You're killing me," McBride said.

Itsuki gave him another tentative kick. "So now we come to these government men you have about you. And the documents."

"One cancels the other," McBride said. "I turned the stuff over to the Feds."

"I do not quite believe that, my friend. It is not like you to part with something valuable for nothing. Perhaps you have told them about me, yes. But about the documents, no."

Beautiful padded in, carrying a brazier full of glowing charcoal. A pair of tongs peeped coyly from the bowl. This can't be real, McBride thought. This is the old Main Street melodrama. Still, he thought, in case it is real, I'm going to be yelling like hell in a minute anyway. Why not yell now?

He yelled bloody murder. Itsuki looked at him in mild amazement. Beautiful, startled, dropped the brazier. A couple of hulking brutes ran in from an adjoining apartment. The one with the gun was not as careful about McBride's feet as Itsuki had been. Bound together though they were, the feet were at the end of a stout pair of legs. They tripped the big guy and he fell against his partner. Both fell on top of the blazing coals.

McBride never took any credit for what happened after that. He knew he couldn't win when he tried for the gun that flew out of the guy's hand. But he did try for it. Arching his back, hands under him, he managed to propel himself off the mat by the time Itsuki stooped for the weapon. McBride suddenly bent the other way and butted Itsuki's head. McBride's must have been the harder of the two, because while he saw a couple hundred stars himself he knocked the little baron out cold. He thought he was still seeing stars, or at least hearing them, when guns started booming outside.

Sweeney came crashing through one of the walls like a clown equestrian through a paper hoop.

"It was like this," Sweeney said. He was very proud of himself. "On account of this hello dame wouldn't give me a tumble I didn't like her anyway, so——"

Miss Ford interrupted him. "You mean the girl on the hotel switchboard? Why, Sweeney, she is a Japanese!"

"So what?" he demanded. "Look, you ever been in the Navy?"

Miss Ford admitted that she never had. McBride's ribald laughter shook the windowpanes. Mr. Cord and Lieutenant Stone said nothing. They were all in Mr. Cord's office in the Federal Building. Outside, the sky was turning a faint pink. It was five o'clock in the morning.

Sweeney continued. "So I don't like this broad, and I get to thinking. Ain't it funny, I think, that there is so many of these brownies around? And ain't it funny that our kidnaping, murdering, thieving pals know what we're gonna do even before we do it?" He looked at McBride. "On account," he explained, "of we run into Mr. Cord's car stalled in the drive, so we know it's no use going down to the fish markets."

Lieutenant Stone coughed. "Get on with it, my man."

"Let him alone," McBride said. "It looks like he was smarter than any of us."

Sweeney became terribly embarrassed. "Aw, it wasn't so much, chief." His eyes glowed briefly. "In a way it was a pleasure. So I says to myself, Sweeney, I says, this dump is probably lousy with spies. And anyway, I says, how the hell could they be holding Miss Ford in a phone booth? I heard her, didn't I? So wherever that first call came from it wasn't no public telephone, it was private. So maybe this skibbie broad has been givin' us all the runaround. Maybe she does know where the call came from. So I go down and beat hell out of her and she does."

Mr. Cord lit the tattered stump of a cigar. "We had quite a time of it for a while. Even after we got the number and the address it seemed unlikely that our friends would be using one of the tea houses. Still, it was worth a try. The neighborhood is a quiet one at night; the tea houses themselves closed." He belched quietly behind a brown hand. "Just the same, if you hadn't started raising merry hell inside we might have been fooled."

"Save it," McBride said. "You don't have to toss any sops to me. I know when I'm licked."

Stone almost choked to death. "I wish to God I could be licked the same way. Nordstrom's got over two thirds of the money left. That makes you what?"

McBride eyed him. "So you've turned honest at last, have you? You admit you'd like a cut?"

"Well——"

McBride nodded. "Maybe you'll get one, pal. Maybe you'll earn it too." He looked at Cord. "I guess I've squared myself with you guys. I don't know about the civil authorities."

Cord speared the cigar butt with a toothpick, so that he could smoke it even shorter. "Admittedly, McBride, you took government business into your own hands in order to advantage yourself and your employers. You permitted a murderer and a spy to roam around loose while you sought to use his accomplice as bait to ensnare her husband. How do you think that will look in a report?"

"Terrible," McBride admitted. "Why put it in?"

Cord threw the cigar away. "Damn it, are you offering to bribe me too?"

"Not at all," McBride said. "We'll both make out reports. I'll send mine in with my income tax. In the Remarks section I'll just mention casually that a cheap private dick and a stumble-bum fighter got something that you guys couldn't get; that you didn't even know existed. That ought to cut at least a couple of years off any rap they hand me. Or don't you think so?"

Miss Ford said, "Rex!"

"I had a dog named Rex once," Sweeney observed.

McBride looked at him. "Was he a good dog?"

Cord banged the top of his desk with a brown fist. "All right, let's get all the stories straightened out! We've got Itsuki and his whole crew. And a nice stink it will make, too, if you ask me. Japan's going to have a sweet time explaining this one."

"What are you going to do about Mrs. Nordstrom?"

"She'll do a stretch."

"A tough one?"

Cord carefully trimmed a new cigar. "What difference does it make to you? In love with her?"

Sweeney said, "With that broad? Hell, no. He's in love with——"

McBride looked at him. "Shut up."

"Well, you are," Sweeney said aggrievedly. He took a bottle out of his inside coat pocket and turned his back.

McBride said, "I told Nordstrom I'd do what I could."

Cord appealed to Lieutenant Stone. "Nice, isn't he? It's a wonder he hasn't got Pearl Harbor in his pocket." He shoved his chair back with a great show of irritation. "According to Mrs. Nordstrom's confession she began by cultivating certain airplane manufacturers. It was peace time. She saw no great harm in that. But from then on it became Army and Navy officers and Itsuki had her in a spot she couldn't get out of. There was some written evidence, something she signed. She reached the point where she would have killed to escape, but killing wouldn't do any good.

"Then came word from her husband. She mentioned a Honolulu trip to Itsuki and he agreed."

Stone said, "Why?"

"Probably for the same reason he moved out of England. It was time for another move and he could use her for a repeat performance here in the Islands."

McBride reached out and took the bottle away from Sweeney. Miss Ford took it away from McBride. He shrugged. "I still don't see why he had to entrust the stuff to her. Why didn't he take it over the side with him?"

"Because a lot of it was not in waterproof ink. Maybe he could have gotten some oiled silk; maybe he just figured he'd let it go through the way he originally intended. His diplomatic immunity might have been questioned. Probably it would have been. But he preferred one chance to the other."

"You guessing all this?"

"Part of it," Cord confessed. "They're still persuading our little brown brother."

McBride looked at Lieutenant Stone. "There was a murder back home that maybe you haven't heard about yet. A maid in the apartment house where Itsuki lived. Itsuki's valet was the kind that liked to break fingers to make people talk. In Lord Fessenden's case the valet was again too zealous. He was becoming a liability instead of an asset. They couldn't get rid of Fessenden's body in time; they couldn't get his blood out of the carpet. Itsuki simply told the guy that if they were caught the best thing to do was the Dutch. The valet did it. Itsuki cheated."

Stone nodded. "That's all pretty well cleared up.